The Invisible Hand

The Invisible Hand

James Hartley

LODESTONE BOOKS

Winchester, UK
Washington, USA

First published by Lodestone Books, 2017
Lodestone Books is an imprint of John Hunt Publishing Ltd., Laurel House, Station Approach,
Alresford, Hants, SO24 9JH, UK
office1@jhpbooks.net
www.johnhuntpublishing.com

For distributor details and how to order please visit the 'Ordering' section on our website.

Text copyright: James Hartley 2016

ISBN: 978 1 78535 498 4
978 1 78535 499 1 (ebook)
Library of Congress Control Number: 2016939767

A CIP catalogue record for this book is available from the British Library.

Design: Stuart Davies

Printed and bound by CPI Group (UK) Ltd, Croydon, CR0 4YY, UK

We operate a distinctive and ethical publishing philosophy in all
areas of our business, from our global network of authors to
production and worldwide distribution.

This book is dedicated to my Mum and Dad.

"The only people who truly know your story are the ones who help you write it."
Ritu Ghatourey

SHAKESPEARE'S MOON

ACT ONE

1

Something Wicked This Way Comes

Hello!

I'm sending you both the same letter, I hope you don't mind.

Dad, I hope this gets to you and that you're safe and not caught up in any trouble out there. Uncle Quentin says he knows someone who told him exactly where you are so I hope you are reading this safe and sound. And, Mum, I hope there is someone there that can read this letter to you. Are you feeling better? More like yourself, I hope. I miss you both a lot but I want you to know that I'm well and happy and I totally understand what you've done and why you sent me here.

Please write to me if you get the chance, or send me a number or address where I can reach you. It would be nice to talk to you both.

So I've been here at St Francis's for almost a month now and I think I'm starting to get the hang of things. I'm in a boarding house called St Nicholas, which is built in the shape of a cross. Some of the boys say that's because it's on the site of an old graveyard but who knows? There are stories about everything here and I don't know what to believe yet. The school is ancient – just like half the teachers and most of the people in the village.

There are five other boys in my dorm (that's where I'm writing this, on my bed, bottom bunk, on the left as you walk in the door) and we all get on. Four have been here since the first year and the other one, Walter, started this year with me. He's cool and we hang about together trying not to annoy the House Quaestors.

Every morning a bell rings at seven and we have to go

outside and run around the block in a pair of shorts even when it's freezing. I don't mind it as it wakes you up but most of the others complain. After the run we shower up and breakfast is at eight. The day bugs start arriving for Assembly at half past and school starts at nine. The food's OK. It's normal school food – big silver trays and soggy veg and all that.

The actual schoolwork is fine too, not much different from Ras Al-Hambra to be honest. We have classes in a place called the Quad and during the boring lessons I read the graffiti on the desks. There's loads of it. People use the desks as a kind of messaging service, which is dead interesting, especially as we're not allowed phones during the week. (Joke, Mum.)

In science we're studying the weather, which is great as the stations are dotted around the edges of the school grounds so it's like exercise too. In English we're reading *Macbeth* and in biology we're doing plant reproduction. Do you think everyone, everywhere in the world, does plant-reproduction in biology? Is there anything else to it?

I play football or rugby twice a week and in the afternoons we have activities like Orientation, which basically means a teacher drops us in the middle of nowhere and we walk around in the woods until the minibus comes back and picks us up.

I want to write more but it's impossible as it's 'lights out' in five minutes. There's so many weird things I want to tell you about. I've learnt loads of new words in these last few weeks, like Exeat, matron, eczema, The Eleusinian Room, Number One Uniform, The Magistrate, tuck, jiving and Prep – this place is like its own world with its own language.

I'm going to sign off now as I can hear the housemaster turning off the lights. He's weird. The boys call him Cyclops because he has a staring eye. His real name's Mr Dahl. He smells weird and looks nasty but he's been fine with me so far.

I miss you both.

Lots of love,
Sam.

2

A Single Event Can Awaken Within Us A Stranger Totally Unknown To Us

It was icy, cold, dark and wet. People were shouting.

Sam thought he'd been carried outside as a joke. Or perhaps it was a fire alarm?

Lifting his head from the cold mud he saw shadows flickering against a pale grey sky. There were stars twinkling through billowing clouds of black smoke. A shadow was moving towards him: a stocky man in a helmet, carrying a sword. "Are ye hurt? Can ye move?"

"Aye, I'm hurt," Sam replied, surprised to hear how deep his own voice sounded.

"Whereaboots?"

"The leg. Below the knee, there."

A moment later Sam felt the pressure against his back and legs ease. "This wan was laying dead astride ye, Rab," grunted the shadowy man, already moving off through the squelching mud. "Move ahn. Move ahn!"

Now that he was able to lift himself, Sam saw he was on a hillside and there were figures carrying scythes and axes moving over the dark ground. A dark, tattered flag was fluttering against the night sky not far ahead of him. He also saw what was pressing down on his legs: a fallen soldier.

It was the first dead body Sam had ever seen: a young man of about sixteen with bits of a beard, closed eyes and an open mouth. His body was dressed in battle armour and blood had dribbled from the corner of his mouth and dried black in his prickly chin hair. Sam stood up and moved off, his boots sinking and sticking in the mud.

This is some kind of battlefield, Sam thought. *I'm dreaming.*

That's all it is. I'm dreaming.

In the spells when the smoke cleared, Sam noticed the sky lightening, turning purple where it bowed to the earth. There was a twinkling stretch of dark water ahead of him upon which thirty warships floated in three rows, their masts and angry figure-heads rocking to and fro on the waves.

"Help me!" came a voice from the darkness to Sam's left. "Somebody, help me!"

"Where are ye?" Sam was too concerned with the search to wonder why he was speaking with a Scottish accent in someone else's voice. Having accepted he was dreaming, nothing seemed strange.

"Here! Over here!"

Sam found the owner of the voice buried beneath two dead soldiers. The survivor was an old man with perfectly white hair, despite the mud and dirt. "Hold tight an' I'll have ye oot in no time," Sam told him.

"This one on top's got his pike jabbed right through mah leg," the man replied, gritting his yellow teeth in pain.

Sam took the news coolly, pulling the first heavy body away before kneeling to examine how he could do the same with the other. As the man had said, the second soldier's weapon had pierced the old man's thigh and the long blade was pinning him fast to the hillside. Sam was about to try and yank out the pike when the old man waved his hands.

"Nay, nay, nay, lad! Snap it, boy, snap it! Snap it and I'll do the rest."

Sam did as he was told, ignoring the man's horrible cries as the wood splintered. After watching him pull the rest of the blade from his leg, Sam hauled the old man up onto his shoulders and started again down the hill. He looked up as the grass and mud turned orange and saw the flotilla of warships alight on the water. Timber cracked as the vessels broke up. Some exploded and one by one they slid beneath the fiery waves.

"Good riddance," growled the old man on Sam's back.

At the foot of the hill Sam was stopped by a captain and directed to a long line of carts roped to mules. Loud groans and cries emanated through the carts' dirty canvass covers as Sam rounded the last in the line. Piled inside were wounded and dying soldiers, some looking sad and tired, others missing arms, legs, eyes or faces.

"Oh, dinnae put me in there," groaned the old man sadly. "I beg ye."

And so Sam limped along behind the carts as they moved off with the old man on his back. *If this is a dream it's a wee bit too realistic*, he was thinking, feeling his twisted ankle and bruised legs throb with each step. The steady weight of the man pressing on his shoulders made his back ache and as the day rose grey and bright, Sam marched with his head bent down to the tyre ruts, thinking of nothing but putting one foot in front of the other.

When he did look up it was to barren countryside: grey-green hills covered with heather and thistle. From gravel slopes rose granite mountains bobble-hatted with mist.

Occasionally they passed through small villages where people in shawls with bad teeth and worse skin came out and offered food or drink or tried to barter. At a busy crossroads a one-eyed farmhand offered to carry the old man for Sam's breastplate and Sam couldn't resist the offer. He climbed up into the wagon of the dead and dying and collapsed on the wooden tailgate.

The path was bumpy, the smell horrendous and the groaning within nightmarish but Sam was so exhausted that within seconds he fell into a profound sleep.

3

Everything You Can Imagine Is Real

The House Quaestors gathered giggling in the shadowy corridor and at a signal from their leader burst into the silent dorms and screamed at the top of their lungs for everyone inside to get out of bed.

Sam didn't know what day or time it was but he was up onto his bare feet on the cold floor and stripped out of his pyjamas in seconds. The buzzing strip light was blinding and it wasn't until he was walking out into the chilly corridor with the others, hugging his bare sides to try and keep himself warm, that his eyes adjusted to daylight.

The seven-o'clock bell rang shrilly as they trudged down through the locker room to the boot room. Here, where their breath smoked and the floor was chilly stone, the boys changed into their running shoes before fumbling outside to where another House Quaestor, dressed and barking orders from behind a thick, green, woollen scarf, checked them off and sent them on their way.

As Sam jogged after the others, trying to ignore the cold gnawing at his ribs and flanks, he glanced across to where sleepy-faced girls were emerging from the Main Building. The junior girls' boarding house was on the second floor and Sam noticed some of the girls had blankets or duvets draped over their shoulders. There was no fraternising or calling out: everyone was too cold or tired to do anything but put one foot in front of the other and keep moving. Each step forward, after all, was one step closer to getting back inside and into the warmth.

The boys' route followed the perimetre of the main lawn and Sam looked up at the branches above hanging bare before the midwinter sky. The puddles he was splashing through were icy-black and frost sharpened the edges of the leaves scraping his numb, red legs. At the school gates he saw senior girls running up the lane opposite and knew they were at their own halfway point. He and his dorm-mates fell into a line and pressed on. They were almost home.

Arriving back, there was a crush at the boot-room door. Oversleepers and their angry friends were trying to push their way outside as Sam and the rest of Dorm Four, arms wrapped around their shoulders, breath steaming, tried to barge past them and get into the warmth.

Sam joined the rush to yank his towel off the racks in the drying room and as quickly as they could they lined up as a dorm to be checked off and let into the showers. With a finite supply of hot water and the House Quaestors already washed, Sam was happy to find that for his thirty seconds under the spray the water was soothingly tepid.

Back in the dormitory, windows steaming up, the boys got changed. Orhan, who'd been at St Francis's since he was eleven, put some music on and they listened as they buttoned their shirts, knotted their ties and finally warmed and woke up.

It wasn't until he was in double maths that Sam remembered his dream. It came back to him like a shattered memory.

Sam and Walter were sitting at the back of the class. Before them were eight rows of bowed heads steadily taking down the quadrilateral equations which Ms Morris was relentlessly scribbling onto the electronic board.

"I had the weirdest dream last night, Walt, man," Sam whispered.

"What about?" Walt pointed out some new graffiti on the desk and sniggered.

Looking up, Sam's eyes caught those of the Welsh teacher and with a jolt of panic he turned back to his notebook. "Tell you later."

"What? You can't start a story and then leave it like that."

"Tell you later, man! Morris's looking!"

As he copied down numbers and pretended to make calculations, Sam tried to think of what might have inspired the dream and made it so vivid. He thought back to the classes the day before: perhaps the talk they'd had in history about Caractacus? What had they been doing in biology? He couldn't remember properly but hadn't it been something about plants? It couldn't have been that, could it?

The day went on and double maths segued into break-time. Walter had to buy something from the school stationers so Sam spent thirty minutes in the locker room at St Nick's watching a nerdy kid called Aldolous play brain games on a tablet. A dreary French class with the ever dour Monsieur Houellebecq, led to lunch and gradually Sam forgot about his dream and so, abandoned, the dream left him.

In double English Mr Firmin had a surprise: they would be going up to the junior girl's common room to watch Polanski's film of *Macbeth*. They could leave their bags in the classroom but they had to bring their copies of the play. As the class walked across the Quad they waved at friends in the other classrooms despite being warned not to. Mr Firmin strolled ahead with his strange, rolling gait causing Mark Smith, a snotty northerner from Dorm Five, to say the way the teacher walked made him seasick.

As they were entering the Main Building during class time everyone, Magistrate or not, was permitted to go in through the main entrance. This was something Sam and most of the others had only ever done with their parents the first time they'd come to the school. At all other times it was strictly forbidden.

Beyond the oak door with the school motto carved into it – *Possunt Quia Posse Videntur* – lay a panelled porch decorated with photographs of staff and students in years gone by. Further in was a large hall with a healthy log fire burning in an ornate grate. Down the corridor to the left was the Staff Room and the mysterious Eleusinian Room, where Quaestors, Praetors and Consuls were initiated into The Magistrate, while in gilded letters, spanning the panels running around the main hall, were the names of every Head Boy and Head Girl the school had ever had.

"Who's got both oars in the water?" Firmin cried as the class grouped up at the foot of the staircase. The English teacher wore a light linen suit and pumps. He had small, birdlike eyes, high cheekbones and a dark, bristly moustache. "Shake a leg over there, chaps! Up we go, please. Lead the way, Mr Kempis!"

In the common room the girls, who were boarders and knew the place, took the good seats while some boys jumped on top of each other on the sofas, play-fighting. Mr Firmin got everyone to settle down and crouched in front of the television dangling a remote control from his hand. "Now how do these blasted contraptions function?" He called Aldolous over and took himself to the window, tucked his fingers in his rope belt and puffed out his broad chest. "I say, what a cracking day!"

Sam glanced about the common room and thought it not much different from theirs at St Nick's. It smelled different though: an odd combination of faraway stale cigarettes and fried breakfasts. There were books piled up along every available shelf and surface, arranged haphazardly, in piles and towers. Here and there were cacti leaning vertiginously in jars in the spaces between the spines.

Directly ahead of where Sam was sitting was a huge bay window. This provided a fantastic view of the back lawns: the fountain, the covered-over swimming pool, the Assembly Hall and, beyond a low fence, the playing fields. Dots of green and white floated about on the hockey pitch. The view disappeared and the room was thrown into darkness as Mr Firmin closed the shutters, yanked the curtains closed and called for everyone to "pipe down".

Within ten minutes of the film starting half the class were asleep, Sam among them.

4

I Decided I Must Be Lots Of Different People Inside My Brain

Sam was shaken awake in the darkness and the first thing he noticed was a foul smell. It was something rotten; like the most rancid bin he'd ever smelled, mixed with the foulest breath, plus fingernail debris and gone-bad wounds.

"You there! Ootta there right this instant!"

Sam saw a warrior brandishing a flaming torch glaring back at him. "Me?"

"Aye, you, mon, you! Who else? Oot!"

Two other men stepped forwards and yanked Sam from the tailgate of the cart and forced him to stand. It was night. "That's the death cart, I'll have ye know. It's nae place tae be sleepin'."

Sam shrugged. "My apologies."

"Name?"

"Cauldhame," replied Sam automatically. He didn't know where the word had come from. The same place as his voice, he imagined.

"Ach! No, you're joking?" The bearded man held the torch so close to Sam's face Sam was sure he could smell his own eyebrows burning. "Rab Cauldhame?"

"The very same."

"With Ross on the battlefield, were ye?"

"Right enough I was," answered Sam. He wasn't sure what he was saying but the words seemed to form without him thinking too much about them. His voice was his own, but deeper. As before, Sam was strangely calm about all this.

"Well, he's gone ahead," the soldier informed Sam, sniffing. "As should ye, like." The stocky soldier rubbed his broken nose as he pondered what to say. "But first I need hands, that's true enough. There's work tae be done here, still." He turned and gestured towards a lonely looking path which disappeared into the smoggy darkness. "Here's what ye'll do, Rab. Ye'll go doon the sooth shore and scoot for bodies. Bring up any ye find. After that ye can make yer ain way hame."

"Aye," nodded Sam. He'd understood that he had to go to the coast but little else.

"Here." The barrel-chested soldier took a bound stick from one of his men, lit it with his own torch and passed it to Sam. "Watch yourself for stragglers, eh?"

Sam took the flaming torch and nodded. "Right, y'are."

"God save the King, Rab."

"Aye. God save the King."

The soldier turned back to the hospital cart and Sam heard him begin shouting at his next victim to wake up and get out. A shadow rose behind the dirty canvas and a groggy voice began remonstrating.

Sam walked off down the narrow path as he'd been told to, his torch raised high above his right shoulder to light the way. The ground was firm and flat and sometimes bright eyes shone at him from the darkness before disappearing in a blink and a rustle. After ten minutes' steady walking he found himself at a cliff edge.

He was above a wide open bay, the sea twinkling out to where a strip of land on the other side lay smudged and obscured by cloud, rain or the night. The sky was coming grey and Sam guessed it was early morning or twilight. Either way he was glad of his torch as he began to scuttle down the steep scree slope, avoiding rocks and crevasses, side footing his way through the dirt and pebbles until he reached the mushroom-like, sea-smoothed rocks which formed a barrier at the top of the beach.

Before he'd had the chance to think about which direction to start off in, Sam heard a woman's voice cry out from somewhere near the low waves dead ahead. Walking out onto the wet, dark sand, Sam saw there was a body on its back in the wrinkling wash. A figure, a woman, rose from beside the body and cried out for help in the same voice he'd heard. Together she and Sam got the dead man up onto the drier sand but it was obvious the wretch was dead. The corpse's face was pale grey and there was seaweed hanging out of the buttonholes of his jacket.

"Are ye with the Thane's men, sir?" asked the woman. She was wrinkled and sad.

"Aye."

"Oh, God be with ye, sir. Help us afore the wreckers come, wiw ya? Be a good soul."

The woman began slipping the rings off the man's fingers and searching the pockets of his coat. Sam was startled by her violent attempts to tear out one of the dead man's earrings. As soon as she had her booty, the woman's face changed. Her black teeth flashed and before Sam could say anything she was off across the sand, leaving small indents which filled with water before they dried.

Sam looked down at the body and out to the sea. Down here the water looked anything but inviting: toffee brown where it rolled in as waves, oily and sharkish where it jagged and chopped against itself out in the bay. The wind was coming up. The taste of rain was in the air. The sky grumbled and the slate-grey clouds passing fast overhead tore apart and reformed in a dance of confusion and Sam thought: *What grim place is this? Why am I dreaming I'm here?*

Looking back towards the cliffs he could see torchlights moving along the rocky summits and remembered his own torch, now only a stick again, extinguished and useless on the sand where he'd dropped it when he'd run to help the old woman.

In his heart Sam felt strangely safe. His spirit, too, was enveloped in a feeling of invincibility and he thought: *I don't know why I'm here but if I keep coming back there must be some reason, some reason I don't know about. I'm only dreaming. I'm only dreaming*. And so he decided to press on, crouching to haul up the body of the drowned man and trudging back up to the dry sand with it draped around his neck like a macabre scarf.

Night was falling now, Sam was sure of that, and cold, changeable winds were beginning to rake the beach. Their snouts and tails cuffed up the loosest sand and whipped it fiercely about. Not being able to see the cliffs anymore, let alone a way up them, Sam thought he saw twinkling lights further down the coast and pressed on despite the conditions. A few minutes later he saw the golden glow of a house which seemed to be cut into the rock and forced himself up the slimy stairs to kick at the wooden door.

Nobody answered.

The wind was almost as loud as the sea now, a raging sea which Sam could hear at his back. Before him, the yellow windows of the house peered out from the steep, dark cliff-face. In desperation he kicked out at the wooden front door again, as hard as his numb feet would allow.

Turning, exasperated, ready to throw the body off his shoulders and into the sea, Sam saw the most beautiful face he'd ever seen in his life staring back at him from behind a thick glass pane at one of the golden windows. It was a girl, about his age, modestly dressed in a shawl which she lifted to cover her nose and mouth as he watched. Her hair, where he could see it, was a rich, chocolate brown. Her eyes were amber. Her skin was pale and somehow infinite.

"Help me," Sam shouted. He turned on the step so the girl might see the face of the man he was carrying.

When he looked back the girl dropped the shawl and mouthed, "Leave him there and go. I beg ye, leave him there and go."

Sam looked into the girl's eyes and could see everything. She was afraid. Someone was in the house with her and she couldn't open the door. They thought he was a wrecker. They were scared of enemy soldiers. They knew the dead man but they wanted nothing to do with Sam. Something in the girl's eyes, something about her, a strong feeling he couldn't well describe, but which was stronger than the wind and the waves and danger, made him to do as she said. He left the body on the upper step and, after one final backwards glance, stepped down to the beach and turned into the wind.

Sam didn't look back.

He would walk as far as he could. Perhaps he would try to climb the cliff.

But the black tide was coming in and soon he was ankle-deep in the freezing waves. They sucked at his ankles and drowned his boots. From time to time he slipped and bruised his wrists and knees. His hands and feet might not have been attached to his body for all he could feel of them. Walking beside the sea that night was like walking next to a vicious creature, something from the underworld, which was snapping and snarling and threatening to devour him, and it took Sam a great mental effort to ignore it and keep moving forwards.

When he could go no further and was tired of wading and swimming, tired of being buffeted against the rocks and swallowing seawater, Sam tried to climb as far as he could up the cliffside. He found a small ledge and curled up in a ball as the icy spray lashed his wet back.

He thought of the girl's face. The vision he conjured up warmed his soul.

5

Game Afoot

"And we'll finish the second half on Thursday," Mr Firmin was saying, rubbing his gnarly hands in a knot.

Sam opened his eyes and quickly, self-consciously, wiped up the drool which had escaped and stained the arm of the old sofa. Beside him Walt Schulberg was stretching and blinking in the light as the wooden shutters were folded over and bright, sunny daylight streamed into the common room.

"Sir, can we stay here now instead of going back to class?" one of the girl boarders asked.

"If you've brought your books and all your kit with you, I don't see why not."

"Lunch," Walt sniffed. "Perfect. I'm starving."

"I just had the weirdest dream," Sam murmured, but no one was listening. He wasn't sure if he was happy to be back at school or sad because the girl he'd dreamed of was just that: a figment of his imagination.

"Sir, next week can we see Macbeth II?"

"I didn't even see this one."

"Go on!" Mr Firmin cried, pretending to try to kick one of the boys on the behind. "Move it, you horrible lot."

Out in the creaking corridor the boys tried to catch a glimpse into the girl's boarding house but the only thing they saw was the housemistress scowling back at them from behind the wire of the fire door. Miss Bainbridge had an unlit cigarette hanging from her mouth. "Scoot!" she mouthed as the boys watched.

The class clumped down the old wooden staircase and fell into a reverent silence as they came to the first landing. At the other end of the well-trodden lime-green carpet they were walking across lay the Headmistress's office. Two glum boys stood with their hands in their pockets outside the closed door and both turned and pretended to look at the aerial photographs of the school on the walls as the class filed by.

"Straight in to lunch?" asked Walt as they came down into the fire-lit main hall.

Sam nodded. "Definitely." But his eyes were drawn up to the list of names of Head Boys and Head Girls running around the boards under the high ceiling. One stood out, immediately catching his eye: *WATERS, ENID*, 1941–42.

Before Sam could read any more, or stop to think about what he'd seen, Firmin was at their backs hurrying them along. The class broke out through the back doors and merged into the queuing throngs impatiently waiting to be admitted to the dining room.

Lunch was dull but Mr Grey's geography class, which followed, was even worse.

It was a blustery October day and Sam's world was a miserable place. One of the heaters in the classroom wasn't working and a kind of creeping cold sneaked its way into Sam's bones as he sat trying to concentrate on coastal erosion in Lanark. Every time he closed his eyes he saw the girl's face imprinted on the darkness in his mind and he couldn't help thinking: *Will I ever see her again?* She had seemed so very real.

The last class of the day was a grim, gruelling double dose of physics. Although he'd managed to somehow wangle his way into the top group in maths and English, in each of the sciences Sam was in the lower group, which meant two hours of staring out at the drizzle whilst listening to the teacher becoming increasingly frazzled by the refusal of half the class to be quiet and listen.

In the top groups most of the students were like Sam. They were fairly well behaved, ultimately afraid of their parents and interested enough to try to do well in the subjects they studied.

Here in the lower groups there were a few lost souls like Sam trying to make the best of things but there was also a hardcore group of boys and girls for whom everything was a joke. Some of them, as the teachers never tired of telling them, were clever enough to get away with this kind of behaviour and still pass their exams, but the majority, they never tired of warning them, would suffer as a result of such behaviour and spoil their chances of success in life.

These laughing, unafraid, rebellious students had fascinated Sam from the first day he'd arrived at the school. The boys had a strange hairstyle all of their own, a kind of crash helmet design, long at the sides and short at the back. It was ugly and dumb-looking but they wore it with a defiance that made it threatening and cool. The girls wore their hair however they wanted but signalled membership of the tribe through their make-up. Mascara patterns swirled off the corners of their eyes and swooped and looped in paisley patterns across the bare skin towards their hair. The most intricate designs stretched right up to their ear lobes.

To these people, Sam was invisible. He watched them and was impressed by them but they were like ants going about their business while he stood staring. Like ants, they had no idea he was even there. Sam, ultimately, was what they might call a "square". He was quiet while they were loud. He was shy while they were proud. Sometimes he felt like he was watching life slip by while those people, dumb as they were, seemed to be actually living it.

That night in Prep he tried to draw pictures of the girl he'd dreamed about because he was starting to worry that he was forgetting what she looked like. When he closed his eyes he could see something, someone, but he wasn't sure if it was her anymore or just an idea he had of her; the her he thought he could remember. A bald, dome-headed teacher in a scarf and hat knocked on the window and Sam looked up. Mr Larkin pointed at Sam's drawing and shook his head, wagging a finger. Sam nodded. *Yes, sir. Sorry, sir.*

Everyone in the room turned to look at him. It was dark outside and the window reflected the buzzing classroom strip lights. The wind, when it came, rattled the old wooden panes. The sixth former sitting at the front desk was glad to not have been caught playing with her phone. "Back to work everyone." She yawned.

Sam waited a few minutes before stretching up to peep out through the window again. On the other side of the foggy Quad he could see Mr Larkin peering into a different glowing window. Sam opened his notebook and began sketching again.

What if I dream of her tonight? It's been two nights now.

Yes. That's what'll happen. I'll dream of her again tonight! I'm going to see her again!

By the time he finally got back to St Nick's Sam was ready to get into his pyjamas and turn the lights out right then and there. He hadn't been as excited about going to bed since Christmas Eve as a kid. He queued for toast and watched television with one eye on the clock. Finally, when the duty HP came into the common room to give them their five-minute warning, Sam could hardly contain his impatience and excitement.

See you soon. See you soon.

In bed he lay listening to the seemingly interminable racket of creaking springs and chattering voices until, finally, painfully late on, the quiet of night descended.

The tawny owl in the oak whose branches spread high over the House roof hooted from its secret perch. From time to time rogue gusts of wind made the great trunk creak and buffeted the prefabricated walls.

It took Sam a long time to fall asleep. He heard coughing. He heard snoring and muttering and teeth grinding. One boy in Dorm Three sat up and began screaming in Hindi. Sam's arms hurt from lying on them. He needed to go to the toilet but knew he couldn't. Finally he went, hating the walk there and back. He lay on his back. He thought of nothing. He thought of home. He thought of schoolwork.

But the magic happened, as it always did, when he wasn't expecting it.

6

What We Think, We Become

Canvas cracked back and forth in the wind like a sail. Sam felt cool air on his face and perceived light on the other side of his eyelids. "Top o' the morning t' ye, Rab," declared a silhouette which appeared in front of him as his eyes flickered open.

Sam pulled himself up onto his elbow and put his hand to his brow. "To ye the same."

"Ye took some blows back there, all right, Robbie, my man. We weren't sure you'd make it there for a wee moment o'tae." Sam looked into the face of a blond, smiling man. Emerald eyes twinkled from the scarred but handsome face. As he stared at Sam a hurt look crossed his face. "You dinnae remember me, do ye?"

"I'm not even sure who I am," Sam answered honestly, and this seemed to satisfy his companion, who laughed loudly.

"Well ye've tae thank yer sister here for nursing ye back tae health," the soldier declared, nodding over Sam's shoulder.

Sam turned and saw the girl. She shone brighter than the daylight. "Aye. Right y'are."

"I did nae ken ye had a sister, Rab." The soldier laughed. "Ya kept that tae yerself, eh?"

The girl of Sam's dreams, truer than life, now smiled at him, bowing her veiled head modestly. "Oh, Rab."

"Well I'm sure we'll be seeing ye both somewhere further doon the line," the blond soldier concluded. "A good morning to ye." He bowed, the weapons hanging from his belt jangling, and left the tent.

Sam smiled, turning to lie on his stomach. "Hello again."

"Hello."

"You know I have to tell you something. I wasn't lying. I really don't know who I am. Or where I am."

"Here." The girl offered him her bent elbow and helped him up off the hard bed. Sam was sore and weak. "Can you stand?" she asked. She spoke with a different accent from the men. Softer. "Your knee was very damaged. Step slowly, now. Try to charge it with your weight."

As they moved with very small steps towards the sunlight, Sam asked, "Where did you find me?"

"On a ledge on the rocks by my master's house."

"And who brought me here? You?"

"Yes. My master wouldn't have you in the house." The girl pulled back the flapping canvas and Sam took in an impressive scene: ranks of soldiers carrying flapping standards and colours, some in armour, some mounted, some pushing war-machines, all lining up in formation under a high, clear, cloudless sky. Around the army was a colourful circus of women, children and animals. The smell of cooking wafted in from the campfires. "I was only there for the night, anyway. I was happy to have an excuse to leave."

"In that case, I'm happy to have been your excuse."

The girl smiled and it was beautiful. "We were put up by the local people after the battle. But it's good to be back here, with everyone."

"What is this place?" asked Sam, in awe.

"The King's camp. We'll ride on to Inverness when you think you're able. Everyone is leaving this morning."

Sam looked at the girl, at the reflection in her eyes, and wanted to close the gap between them. It was difficult to know what to say. "What's your name?"

The girl narrowed her eyes and pursed her mouth to speak. Two soldiers carrying armfuls of shot came bumbling through the guy ropes of their tent and called out a hearty good morning.

"Go ahn, Rab," the girl told Sam, in a loud voice obviously meant for the others to overhear, her accent suddenly strong.

"Get ye yer bread, cheese and bacon. I'll prepare the mounts, don't ye worry."

"Aye." Sam nodded, realising the game. He lifted the canvass flap, hobbling into the sunlight proper.

"Oh, Robbie?"

"Aye?"

The girl walked over to Sam, leaned up on tiptoes and whispered in his ear, "It's Leana."

Sam wasn't slow in finding out that Robbie Cauldhame was a popular man. Everyone wanted to shake his hand and pat him on the back; most seeming to have given him up for dead. Sam's strangeness and awkwardness was attributed to Robbie's war-wounds. The King himself, Sam told Leana as they led their horses up the busy track towards the main road, had said he wanted to see him when they reached Inverness. His Highness wanted to see all the veterans; all the survivors. "This is all so odd," Sam concluded breathlessly. "I mean, how far away from here is Inverness?"

Leana wheeled around and warned him sharply, under her breath, "Not another word until we're alone." Sam was shocked to see she was red in the face. Her eyes flickered to the soldiers and families walking nearby. "Watch your tongue, eh, boy? Or do you want to have us both hung?"

"Hung?" Sam pulled a face, but he was cold with shock. "That's a bit much."

"Oh aye, it's a bit much. Because you *know*," replied Leana, nodding. "You know best." She walked on ahead. "That's right."

Of course I'd probably know how far Inverness was from here, Sam thought as they trudged on. He felt like a bairn waddling after it's mammy. *Robbie Cauldhame would know.* They reached the main road without exchanging another word. Leana was always a stride or two ahead and at the post house on the crossroads she made him wait while she went for their horses. Sam took the worn leather reigns in his big ugly hands. *And I'd know how to ride.* He tried to smile at Leana when she came back but she wouldn't look him in the eye.

"I lead," Leana declared, obviously still angry. She pulled her mare's snorting head around and clicked her tongue. "Stay close, boy. Try not to fall off, eh?"

They trotted in file through the stinking remains of a temporary village – sewage, excrement and churned mud splashing up to their boots and the horses' bellies – picking up speed as they set off across a wide valley where the way was marked by occasional mile-posts. Sam spotted circling eagles, a lynx, elks, a sleeping pack of wolf cubs, possibly dead, and a single, mangy brown bear wandering along the pebbly shore of a small loch.

After three hours riding, climbing slowly into the highlands, they hit banks of fog which reduced their visibility and speed. At nightfall, because Leana said she wanted to go as far as possible, they rode up to a wider road pocked with inns whose lantern lights stretched out into the darkness like lights across a midnight sea.

Sam had expected them to stop at one of the inns but to his disappointment they soon turned off the road again into bare, rugged, pitch-black country and rode closely together for what seemed like hours. Just when Sam thought he was about to drop with exhaustion he noticed Leana pulling up the reins.

"Is this it?" he asked, stretching his arms up over his head, sore all over. They had stopped at a deserted stone cottage whose windows were darker than the night. It didn't look like a castle, more like a glorified outhouse, half-collapsed.

Leana was watering the steaming horses. "No, of course it isn't. I wanted to talk to you alone before we got to the castle."

"Yes. It would be nice to talk." Sam pointed at a nearby structure which seemed to shine in the night air. "Is that a well?"

"It was but don't drink from it. It was poisoned in the war."

Leana put her hands on her hips and took a long breath, cool air smoking from both nostrils.

"How long are you going to be angry with me?"

Leana had her head bowed. She looked up with steady, accusing eyes. "Well, perhaps until you tell me who you are?"

"I see." Sam nodded and placed his hands on his own hips. He thought about his answer. 'I'm Sam', should he say? Or 'I'm Robbie'? Was he in danger? Could he trust this girl? "I don't know," was what came out. "I'm sorry but that's as close to the truth as I can get. I just don't know."

"Are you evil?"

"No!"

"Good?"

"I don't know!" Sam shrugged. "I'm not really anything. I'm normal." He threw out his arms. "I think I'm dreaming. But it's been three nights now, so maybe I'm not. It seems to happen when I'm asleep, so that's why I think I am. But I go back in the middle, you see. Back to normal."

"You were dead." Leana was upset. She prodded a finger at him, her eyebrows furrowed. "When I found you. On the rocks. Stone dead. No heartbeat. Yet when I dragged you back to the house you revived. I had to get you out before they threw you in the sea. They said you were a daemon!"

"I think I'm in a dream," Sam repeated. "When I fall asleep I come here. Maybe I bring someone to life when I come – I don't know! Perhaps I'm in your dream?"

Leana, hands still firmly planted on her hips, tilted her head back, obviously not believing a word of what he said. In that instant, though, her eyes shifted to Sam's shoulder, to whatever she saw there, and they widened with horror and surprise. Her appearance changed completely. Something seemed to have scared the life out of her. "Oh, no! Not now!"

Sam looked back over his shoulder and stared into the dark fog. He saw nothing but felt a presence. His skin went cold and his scalp seemed to shrink. "What is it?" Instinctively he took a step towards Leana, and she to him. It crossed his mind that there might be someone in the fog who wished to do him harm: the presence he'd felt had been malevolent. Had she brought him here to do away with him? It was the perfect place for a murder.

"They're here," Leana whispered, her voice hoarse. "They're here again."

Faces formed in the fog: laughing, cackling female faces which circled them with long, smoky necks which wisped and vanished.

"What are they?" Sam asked. He was transfixed by the visions which broke apart and formed again in the mist.

"Be this your prize, your game, your trial?" hissed one empty black mouth with the voice of a thousand serpents. As it spoke, oval eyes manifested and glowed lizard yellow.

"Be love's young dream," crowed another sarcastically.

"Ripe and fine," growled the last as the two first laughed in a horrible chorus.

"Perfect place."

"Perfect time."

"'Til Selene's eyes blink thrice!" the snake-mouthed one cried. "We'll fly, we'll fly!"

"And you'll show us, so, if love is blind."

"Or if it can survive both fate and time."

The faces faded and the fog settled to form an unbroken bank.

"Oh, I should have let the master drown you!" Leana threw off Sam's arm and cried out in anger and desperation, stomping over to the horses and unwrapping their reins.

"What? Oh, that's lovely." But as Sam approached, Leana screamed.

"No! Stand back, sir!"

"Leana – please!"

But Leana spoke quickly, climbing up into the saddle. "The castle, if that's truly where you're headed, is on the main path –

turn north at the crossroads. Ride hard. Do not come off the road." She wrapped her scarf around her face and knotted it angrily. "I beg you not follow me, sir. I beg you return to hell where you belong!" Leana's heels ground into her horse's flanks and the mare sprung up in pain. "Yah!"

Sam heard the horse's hooves galloping away long after he lost sight of her.

Beside him, treading nervously, his own horse whinnied. Sam held out his hand to calm her. "You know I'm not bad, don't you, girl?"

As he told himself to climb back up into the saddle, wearying at the thought of the pain that act would cause, Sam noticed a figure emerging from the fog bank, walking towards the well. He thought it was Leana returning and was about to call out to her when he realised it wasn't. The walking woman, ethereal and grey, almost transparent, was older than Leana, not as pretty but strong and handsome nevertheless. She was also carrying a baby wrapped up in swaddling clothes.

As Sam looked on the woman walked slowly to the well and placed the baby into the wooden pail hanging from the pulley. Sam could see right through the woman's shape: he could see trees on the other side of her and the rocks piled up alongside the edge of the path. Was the vision a ghost? Was she somehow connected to the visions in the fog; the witches?

The woman looked over her shoulder once before using the handle to lower the pail with the baby down into the well. Her strong, pretty face crumpled and became noticeably younger as the rope unwound.

When there was no more rope the woman knelt by the well and wept. When she finally stood up she was stoic and poised. She turned to where Sam had seen the witches' faces, lifted her arms and seemed to call out silently into the fog. A moment later she turned and walked away, segueing into the fog, her cloak drawn up over her head, arms buried within a single sleeve.

Feeling the heightened atmosphere return to normal, Sam walked across to the well but found the rope end dangling from the mangle frayed and broken. There was no pail and, looking down into the gloom, he saw no child. The well smelled of sulphur.

Without further ado he saddled up and rode away as fast as he could.

7

All Rests On Perseverance

Sam made for the road. By now he was convinced he was in a series of very real, extremely vivid dreams; dreams so deep they were impossible to wake from, but dreams nevertheless.

The strange scene at the well had provoked different emotions. The apparitions in the fog had chilled him but he hadn´t felt scared. What had moved him most was Leana, the way she had reacted to him and the way she made him feel. He felt an overwhelming urge to try to find her and explain himself to her: to show her who he was. She was the only thing that seemed real in this whole ugly, cold, dark dream-world and it hurt him to know that she thought he was a monster. To convince her that she was wrong about him seemed the thing he had to do: the thing he wanted to do. That was what his dream was about, he was convinced.

At the crossroads, just as Leana had said, and despite the fog and moonless night, Sam saw a glow on the northern horizon. He rode towards it and gradually made out the torches of a crowd gathered outside a mighty but forbidding castle which rose above a steep, stubby motte.

Nearing the multitude Sam was challenged and identified himself, dismounting and allowing a hooded, hopping, one-legged peasant to lead his horse away. He joined the last ranks of the parade line trailing back from the drawbridge, nodding to anyone who acknowledged him. The other soldiers seemed pleased he'd made it and he was welcomed into the fold as one of them, just as he had been at camp. A few moments later there was a loud flourish from the castle walls and a screeching as the portcullis was wound up. This was the signal for the royal parade to move forwards and begin entering the castle.

As they walked through the entrance arch into the castle proper Sam looked up at the murder holes ready to disperse oil or tar on invading armies but which were now mercifully empty. He filed slowly past the heavily armed guards lining the route into an open courtyard and took his place in the rows lining up behind the King who was busy taking the salutations of the castle's master and his staff.

As forbidding as the outside of the fortress had been, the atmosphere within was lighter. The forecourt had been decorated for the royal visit and as they entered the delicious smelling feasting hall the soldier's eyes lit up. The long tables had been set for the state banquet and smiling servers were standing, bowing and curtseying, with jugs of mead and ale. Hooded cooks busied themselves with final preparations, passing in and out of the steaming kitchen while an enormous red-faced woman tended to a fat pig suspended over a spitting fire at the far end of the hall.

To another flourish of trumpets, a strong, handsome woman with flying, flowing hair came striding down the central passageway and called out to the King, "Your Majesty!"

"Macbeth's better half," Sam's companion whispered to him.

"To all of you fighting men and your parties, the warmest of welcomes," the mistress of the castle called out, and a cheer went up from the ranks. "I implore you one and all to drink and eat your fill! You've all earned it!"

Porters and aides unburdened the soldiers of coats and shawls and showed the men and women of the royal party to their places. Plates and glasses were charged. Standing for a toast, Sam spotted Leana between the strolling players singing in the aisle. She had her back to him and was sitting near the north end of the hall, close to the now closed doors. There was no chance to speak to her during the meal and when he did look back later on he was sad to see she'd gone.

When the meal and dancing were over, Sam followed his guide's flickering torchlight across the chilly courtyard and up the cold, stone, wind-raked steps to the castle's private apartments. He was happy to find a fire had been lit in his room. "You're on the same floor as my master," the hunchbacked attendant chattered as he lit the two lamps on the wall. "Twixt your sister and my master's chamber, so you are. Twixt the two, in the middle like a filling."

"My sister sleeps nearby, you say?" asked Sam.

The attendant put a finger to his lips. "Two or three rooms away, one way or the other." A simpleton's smile told Sam everything he needed to know about the man's intelligence. "Down or up. Left or right. 'Tis all the same, in the end, ain't it? Depends which way up you are to start with, eh?" This, seemingly, was a great joke. "We're down to the clouds, after all, aren't we, sir?"

Sam bade the servant goodnight and was disconcerted to see a masked man standing at the top of the staircase outside the room brandishing a scythe. Closing and locking his door, Sam's first thought was to leave any attempt at contacting Leana until morning but there was a niggling desire in him to see her right away. He knew he wouldn't be able to sleep without talking to her, or at least trying to. He felt he needed to sort things out – to show her who he really was. But how?

Sam procrastinated for so long the fire shrank to a heap of ash with a thousand red eyes. When he rose from his bed he went over to the window and unjammed the half-frozen lock with the buckle of his belt. An almost full moon, slowly being eaten by the shadow of the sun, shone high above the land-moored fog. Sam had a clear view of the silver, magical countryside right out to where the snow on the far off mountains hung in the night like slithers of heaven. Looking down, breathing clouds of grey air, Sam saw a small stone ledge which he thought might hold his weight.

What are you doing, Lawrence?

Sam climbed out of the window carefully, quietly, the cold wind blowing up his shirt and making him shiver, his fingers whitening on the ledge as he hung down and tried one toe first. The ledge took.

Slowly he lowered both feet onto the stony outcrop, his full weight, and perceived the long drop down to the icy moat between his legs and felt dizzy. The ledge was so narrow he had to have his forehead and chin pressed hard against the stone wall while his fingers remained curled around the window sill.

Don't look down.

Very carefully Sam began to edge his way across the bare wall. The masonry was freezing to the touch but thankfully jagged and imprecisely laid. There were handholds and nooks and crannies and – as he neared the window he hoped was Leana's – he placed his fingers in one such a hole and disturbed an owlet, which screeched as it flew out past his head, almost knocking him off the wall.

Stay calm! Stay calm!

Sam drew himself alongside the window and heard voices within. The metal jamb was slightly ajar, the window tilted away from him. People were whispering: a man and a woman. Sam grew jealous thinking he was overhearing Leana speaking to another man but as he listened more closely he realised what he was hearing were the voices of the master and mistress of the castle.

Thinking of turning back, Sam became aware of Lady Macbeth's voice directly above him at the window. He closed his eyes, sure she would look down and catch him. "Ah, infirm of purpose!" she was hissing. "Give me the daggers!" A moment later Sam felt what he thought was rain against his face. Looking up he saw two glinting knives against the face of the moon: some kind of liquid from the knives had dripped onto his face.

Sam became dizzy again. The conversation he'd overheard, the goo he was examining on his hand – *blood! blood!* – the height and the coldness and the hour and the ordeal became too much for him.

His fingers simply left their holds and he tumbled down through the air with his eyes wide open, not saying a word.

8

The Man Who Has No Imagination Has No Wings

Mr Dahl the housemaster was squinting at Sam with his one good eye. "Are we awake, Mr Lawrence?"

Sam heard a tiny electronic beep sound somewhere under his chin and a person sitting beside Mr Dahl, whom Sam could smell but not see, reached towards him and took something from under his arm.

Sam's eyes weren't working. The room was fuzzy.

"Thirty-nine and a half," read the old lady, and Sam recognised her voice. It was the matron, Mrs Risden.

"Dose him up," stated Mr Dahl. The bed unsprung as the housemaster stood up.

Sam realised he was in Sick Bay, a place he'd heard about. It was a small room off the corridor which led from the common room to Mr Dahl's apartments. As the matron came back with a syringe of something red, Sam cocked his eyes to the left and saw there was another bed nearby with someone in it.

He swallowed the medicine. "Try and sleep," croaked the matron, in a voice neither tender nor rough.

When she'd gone Sam looked over at the pile of sheets on the other bed and whispered, in a very unsteady voice, "Leana?"

But instead of a pretty girl, a snub-nosed Indonesian boy called Pramoedya turned to him. "What you want, freak?"

"Pram? What are you doing here?"

"Me ill. You?"

Sam laughed and shivered. "Me too. Obviously."

"I nearly better. Don't cough on me. You stay your side."

Sam sat up. "It's so cold in here."

"Window open little bit," Pram replied. He'd turned back to

the wall. "And you ill. It's not so cold. You ill. You need air."

"Maybe," Sam croaked. He lay back on the wet pillow. "Oh, I feel terrible. Everything hurts."

"Later, when you feel good, want go outside, you close window. Not now. They come back in one hour for take temperature again. Now we sleeping. Later you close little window when you want go out, OK? Now we sleep."

Sam closed his eyes. He didn't understand a word. He had a headache. Everything hurt. He couldn't stop shivering. "Great. Thanks, Pram."

"Now you shut mouth."

Two days later Sam was released, on unsteady legs, back into the wild.

As he and Walt were queuing with the rest of the school to go into Assembly that morning, Walt surprised him with some news: "I've got a girlfriend." Her name was Salma and she was in the year below theirs. Sam wasn't sure what the right reaction was to this news was and so said nothing. As they sat in Assembly he thought about Leana and realised that he hadn't dreamed or seen her in almost four days. *Perhaps because I was ill I couldn't see her?*

That night, his first back in Dorm Four since his Sick Bay hiatus, Sam prepared himself for a journey back into Leana's world. The last thing he could remember was falling from the ramparts of Macbeth's castle; Leana had been in another room. Perhaps he would wake up on the ground and have to climb back up. Perhaps it would be morning. Whatever happened he was excited about the idea of seeing her again. He'd missed her.

Sam tried to zone out the chatter: some of the older boys had begun to sneak outside at night, exploring the school in groups and coming back to the dorms in the early morning. The housemasters and other teachers knew nothing about this and some of the boys in Sam's dorm were thinking of joining in. A discussion was underway which went on for what seemed like hours. Finally, around midnight, there was a tapping on the window but all the boys except Sam were asleep. Whoever it was left quickly and at last Sam could concentrate on trying to get to sleep.

But sleep wouldn't come.

He began to notice odd noises: the arhythmical ticking of Walt's wristwatch hanging down from the bunk above him. The snores from someone in Orhan's bunk: Orhan or Femi, the Nigerian who said he was a prince. The bed was uncomfortable. He needed the toilet and padded down to the bathrooms along ice-cold floors, remembering only when he got to the urinals that he hadn't worn his slippers. Getting back into bed he thought about his dirty feet. Then about Leana. Then about sheep.

At some point he dreamed, or slept, but it was a muddled dream of swans and magic buses you could enter through gaps in the number plates, and which could fly, which itself was interrupted by the hammering of the morning bell.

Sam sat up in his bunk with an awful, thick head and looked upon the scene of the others waking up as if it were a joke, as if they were all playing a joke on him. It couldn't really be the morning, could it? Why was he still here?

As they stood to queue to run outside, all together, the mist heavy and thick on the lawns, Sam became very sad. It was a sickening sadness that gripped him, far worse than any homesickness he'd suffered. It was a cold white pain which almost blinded him. It really had all been a series of dreams. He would never see Leana again. Nothing special had happened. Nothing special would ever happen.

It had all been a dream.

He fell asleep in French that morning and would have fallen asleep in English too if it hadn't been for the subject matter of the class. "Act Two, Scene Two!" Firmin bellowed from his desk. Mr

Firmin was in fine form, eyes twinkling, moustache bristling, taking large inhales of breath beside the window. "Ah, this weather! *That time of year thou mayst in me behold...*"

"Page twenty-six." Walt prodded Sam.

Sam was lifeless and depressed. He flicked open his copy of *Macbeth*.

"Miss Hunt, you'll be Lady Macbeth," Mr Firmin declared. "And Samuel, you'll be her husband."

Sam groaned inwardly. He looked behind himself at Violet, the prettiest girl in the class, but she was whispering to her companion, a day girl who looked just like her but was slightly less striking.

"Johan Fitzgerald, perhaps you'd like to remind us about what's just happened?"

"Er, the King's dead, sir?"

"Good. And who killed him?"

"Macbeth, sir?"

"Good. Why, Lydia?"

"Because he wanted to be the King, sir."

"Good. Anything else?"

"Because his wife told him to, sir."

"Good. And why do he and Lady Macbeth think they have a right to be King and Queen of Scotland? Anyone?"

"Because the witches told Macbeth he'd be King, sir."

"Good." Mr Firmin snapped closed his book. "So. Here we are, then. Macbeth's castle. Enter Lady Macbeth." Quietly the teacher shooed Violet Hunt to speak.

"That which has – no, have – no, hath – made them drunk," Violet began. "Hath made me bold. What hath cleansed."

"Quenched," corrected Firmin, bending at the knees and raising a balled fist.

"Quenched. What hath quenched them. H-h-hath given me fire."

"She's drunk!" bellowed Mr Firmin, grinning. "And now: An

owl shrieks!"

"Hark. Peace," began Violet monotonously.

"That was me!" Sam shouted. There was a silence. Sam had a grin on his face which stretched from cheek to cheek. "Yes! I swear! That was me! I was there. I climbed the tower. I was looking for someone." Why should he be ashamed? "I was looking for Leana and I made the owl shriek. I scared it, by accident."

Mr Firmin impersonated a goldfish as he rocked on his heels and the class began to laugh.

"He's been ill, sir," Walt said, chair screeching as he pushed it back. "I'll take him to matron."

"Excused," nodded Mr Firmin, quickly electing a new Macbeth.

"He was there," echoed Lucy, putting her hand over her mouth and giggling.

The following week in Assembly Sam was surprised to hear his name read out. He was among the list of boys who were asked to report to the Headmistress's office.

Once again he'd slept badly, hardly at all. Paradoxically this world, the school, had taken on the aspect of a dream for Sam, especially with the current misty, foggy weather they were having. Days merged into nights and nights into days and all was a blur to Sam. Nothing seemed to matter.

After collecting his bag from the house, he walked with his friends towards the Quad but split off to go in to the Main Building as the others wished him luck. There was a fire in the grate in the hall and some of the teachers coming out of the staff room cast suspicious eyes at him. But as soon as they saw he was walking up the staircase to the green-carpeted hallway and the office at the end of it they left him alone.

Sam joined a queue of three at Mrs Water's door. One by one the students disappeared inside, emerging chastised and silent.

Finally, it was Sam's turn and he knocked once, as he knew you must, before he let himself in.

Mrs Waters – nicknamed Hachet Face, or simply Hachet – was sitting at a large desk in front of a semi-circle of bright bay windows which looked out over the back lawns and vast playing fields. "Good morning, Samuel. Come in and have a seat."

Closing the door, Sam was careful to avoid banging the handle against the edge of a packed bookshelf which ran the length of the back wall. He walked past a three-piece leather suite and vaguely remembered sitting on it between his father and uncle about a year previously. There was a painting of a tall man with a large, almost human-looking black cat hanging on the right-hand wall – this was Professor Wolland, St Francis's first Headmaster – and opposite, above the fire, a portrait of a much friendlier looking ex-headmaster with grey hair and a pug.

"Come on, come in, I haven't got all day. Park yourself here, please, Mr Lawrence."

When he sat down Sam could see Mrs Waters properly, close-up, for the first time since he'd been at the school. She was a prim, tidy, black-eyed English woman with old-fashioned clipped good manners and short, bobbed hair. Sam was used to seeing her in Assembly, on the dais behind a lectern, and it was disconcerting to see her so near. She was wearing white make-up which made her look as though she were wearing a mask and could have been any age from sixty to eighty.

"Well," the Headmistress began with a sigh. "There's no point beating about the bush. We're rather worried about you, Samuel." Something happened to her ruby lips, some kind of spasm, which might have been a smile, but they quickly fell straight and thin again before Sam could decide quite what it was. "You seem to be rather suffering with your health, my boy. Care to explain?" Mrs Waters cocked her head. "Perhaps you'd like to tell me what you think?"

"Well, miss –" Sam didn't know what to say – "I've been ill."

"Sleeping well?"

"Yes, miss."

Mrs Waters waited a moment and then picked up a piece of paper from her desk. It was covered with blue scrawls. "It's come to our attention that you've been exhibiting some rather worrying behaviour, Samuel. I have reports here from various members of my staff. Where is it? Ah, yes. It says here that you've been voicing various ideas you attribute to a series of dreams you have been having?" She took off the glasses she'd put on to pretend to read the note. "Would you care to tell me anything about this?" The Headmistress faked confusion. "I can't make head nor tail of it."

"I haven't been feeling well," Sam replied. Instinct stopped him from adding further details. "I get confused."

"I see." Mrs Waters interlinked her knuckles on the desktop. "Now your father is on a dig abroad, isn't he?"

"Yes, miss."

"Somewhere in the Middle East?"

"That's right, miss." Sam sniffed. "Not sure where."

"And your poor mother?"

Sam shrugged. "They say she's better, miss. I haven't seen her for a while."

"You know I have many of her books," Mrs Waters said, gesturing towards the bookcase at the back of the room. "Such a shame what happened to her. A very talented writer. It must have been very hard for you not knowing where she was for so long."

"Actually I spent last summer with my father," Sam replied. "I didn't hear about it until I got back to England." He was uncomfortable with the subject. If he could have put his feelings into words he might have said 'this is none of your business' to Waters but instead he forced a smile. "But, yes. We're happy she was found, miss. Hope she gets better quick."

"Quickly," corrected Mrs Waters, thinning her already thin

lips. "Yes, I followed the whole incident in the newspapers." Mrs Waters seemed to enjoy watching him squirm. "Terribly sad."

"Hopefully she'll get better soon," Sam answered robotically.

"But she's recovering now, you say?"

"Yes, miss. I think so, miss."

"Her memory?"

"I think so, miss."

"Her mental state?"

"Yes, miss."

"Because she's mentally ill, isn't she, Sam?"

"That's what they say, miss." Sam added, "Just an episode, miss."

"Mental illness," repeated Mrs Waters, nodding sagely, taking a long, dramatic breath. "And do you know when you'll be allowed to see her?"

"At half-term, I think, miss. When my father comes."

Mrs Waters sighed again and tried to look sympathetic. "All of this must have taken a terrible toll on your own mind, Samuel; on your own emotions. Your mother going missing and then being found. Her illness. Your father so far away. And moving here, to St Francis's. To a new school. New people. New places."

"It has been hard, miss, yes, but I like it here."

Mrs Waters' lips thinned again. "I see." She turned to the computer screen. "Your legal guardian is your uncle, I see here?" Her eyes flickered to Sam's. "Mr Burgess?"

"That's right, miss."

"Well." Mrs Waters sighed. "I have to tell you, Samuel, that if this worrying behaviour continues and if you feel you can't talk to me or any of your tutors or teachers about it, it seems to me that the only course of action left open to us is to inform your parents and see if we can't get you some professional help."

"Yes, miss."

"You have nothing more to say, I see?"

Sam shrugged. "No, miss."

"You know it'll do you no good to keep everything in your head, my boy. It's far better to talk." She raised an eyebrow. "Or write it down, perhaps? If that comes easier?"

"Thanks, miss. I'll see."

"Have you been writing?" Miss Waters asked, her face suddenly darkening. A strange kind of yellow, lizardish light flashed in her eyes. *Perhaps that was why strange things were happening to the boy*, she suddenly thought. *Perhaps he had the power?*

"No, miss."

Miss Waters examined Sam but seemed satisfied. "Very well. Then I sincerely hope I don't see you again for a very long time."

"Thanks, miss. Me too."

"Off you go, then."

Sam did his best to control himself for following few days and, in fact, he did feel better. He slept well most nights and had no more dreams about Leana or her world. He did his best to pay attention in class, or at least to *seem* to pay attention, and in English he was silently grateful to Mr Firmin for not choosing him to perform if and when they studied *Macbeth*. His classmates found other things to laugh at and other people to pick on and his 'I was there!' outburst was soon forgotten. Sam put it down to illness and lack of sleep and came very close to forgetting it himself.

Each term was broken up into two Exeats and a Half-Term week. An exeat was a weekend when everyone, even the boarders, were supposed to leave school and stay with their guardians, parents or friends. Of course, some unlucky souls had no one to stay with and the school ran a minimal service for those who were stuck inside, but Sam, for his part, had been looking forward to a weekend at Uncle Quentin's to escape and recharge. So he was more than disappointed when on the Thursday before

Exeat his uncle phoned to tell him that because of work it was impossible for Sam to come for the weekend and that he'd have to stay in school. "I promise I'll make it up to you at half-term, buddy," Uncle Quentin had concluded with genuine hurt and regret in his voice. "You know I wouldn't do this if I could avoid it."

And so Sam faced the awful prospect of being trapped in a near-abandoned school for a whole weekend while everyone else got some time out in the real world. He thought briefly of running away but the October weather was cold and drizzly and the thought of lying under branches, in mud or on wet leaves was worse, if anything, than being stuck in an empty St Nick's.

The Friday before Exeat was the worst day, having to listen to everyone talking about where they were going to go and what they were going to do. Worse, when he came back from lunch he was told that he and the only other boy who was not leaving – as fate would have it, Pram the Indonesian – would have to sleep together in Dorm One, usually the domain of snivelling, homesick First Years.

The rain was falling during the last class of the day, music, when Walt attempted to cheer his mate up. "You want to be careful, Sammo. Full moon tomorrow, isn't it? You know what that means? All the Satanists out. All in their robes, wandering into the abandoned school, looking for virgins."

Sam banged his head on the desk. "I hate you."

Walt chuckled. "Ah, come on, man. It'll be all right. They're not going to stop you going out. You can go up the shop. Watch whatever you want on telly. Stay up as late as you want. Go for walks. It'll be over before you know it." Walt stared out the window at the pouring rain. "And you never know, this might clear up too."

"It's going to be the longest two days of my life," Sam moaned.

Both boys turned as the irritating tinkling at the piano, which had been going on for twenty minutes, abruptly stopped. They could hear Mr Theroux, the music teacher, clapping his hands and trying to quieten everyone down. Only the presence of Mrs Waters, face porcelain-white under an enormous, dark umbrella, brought discipline to the proceedings.

"Guys," Mr Theroux said, re-entering the room after a brief interview with the Headmistress. He was red and embarrassed at having been caught presiding over such a chaotic class. "It looks like we have a new student. So, come on, let's give a big, warm welcome to…"

"Leana," whispered Sam, almost falling off his chair in shock as he saw the new girl standing in the doorway.

9

Love Your Enemies

There was no chance for Sam to get any information about Leana during what remained of the music class. He caught a glimpse of her as she left the room through a bank of winter coats and shoulder-straining backpacks and thought she looked remarkably relaxed and composed. This left him wondering if it really was his Leana at all. Their eyes had met as she'd first been introduced, he'd thought, but maybe he'd imagined that as well?

He had Salma, Walt's girlfriend, to thank for more concrete information. This was acquired as they all shivered in the queue for dinner, huddled together in the spitting rain on the wrong side of the dining-room windows. Winter was settling in now, howling the wind down the front of the Main Building and seeping through tights, socks and trousers to settle inside growing young bones. Mini rucks had broken out in the rush for heaters in the classrooms and girls were permitted to wear woollen scarves to class. In the very early and very late periods, the teachers had begun to ignore fingerless gloves.

"The poor thing's just been dumped here because she's got no family," Salma explained. "Her mum and dad were, like, doctors, working with refugees in Africa or Syria or somewhere, and they drowned when one of the boats they were on went down. They had to move her here because her grandmother couldn't cope. And now she's stuck here. She can't even go out this weekend, imagine. The only one in the whole house who's stuck in for exeat! Bainbridge is screwing because it means she has to stay in and keep the heating on. She likes it cold, you know. Like a freezer, because it reminds her of her messed up childhood."

As they filed into the dining hall and mash was dolloped onto his plate and soup ladled into his pale-blue bowl, Sam felt his spirits rising for the first time in weeks.

Leana would be at school all weekend, practically alone with him. Trapped.

Perfect!

Things couldn't have worked out better. Instead of kneeling up at the common room window like a dog left at home, the next morning found Sam waving off Walt and his housemates with the cheeriest of smiles. The front lawns and red tiles of the Main Building were sprinkled with a hard, scratchy frost, which refused to melt and promised ever-colder weather, but the morning was bright, the sky clear for the first time in days, and there was even a faint blur of a faraway sun trying to gleam down from somewhere behind the hazy, high-up clouds.

Sam was dressed for winter, in boots, scarf and a thick coat. He purposely scuffed the ice and frost as he made his way through the sea of bags, cases and children flooding the busy driveway. Since childhood he'd never been able to resist kicking snow or autumn leaves. It was just one of those strange things he always did, like pulling faces in the mirror if he was alone in an elevator.

Once he'd walked around to the back of the Main Building Sam wandered conspicuously out over the lawn to the frozen pond between the Assembly Hall and silently prayed Leana would see him from one of the windows of the junior girls' house.

Sure enough, when he turned back towards the Main Building a few minutes later, there she was. A pair of dark eyes, unmistakably hers, stared out at him from between a thick brown bobble hat and a green woolly scarf.

"Hello again," Sam said.

"Hello," Leana answered.

"Your voice sounds weird." Sam had his hands in his pockets and was twisting his toecaps into the frosty grass.

"So does yours."

"This is my normal one."

Leana smiled and lit up. "This isn't my normal one!"

"Shall we go for a walk? We need to talk, right?"

Leana nodded and they moved off towards the Assembly Hall. Behind the building they joined a short, winding path which passed by the tennis courts and finished at the edge of the vast playing fields. The grass was a white totality, so uniformly pale that it camouflaged the far-off goalposts. The tall, proud elms, which formed a small copse between the cricket squares and the furthest pitch, gave them something to aim for and they crunched off together in its general direction. A trail of snowy footprints connected them with the path they'd left.

The countryside, which surrounded the school, was pretty: a panoramic wintery scene animated by birds breaking from the tree canopies and sailing into the blue sky. But for their steps and breaths, all was silent.

When Sam looked up at the far-off hills a strange phenomenon occurred. The boys called it 'the conveyor belt', a weird feeling of not actually moving as you walked across the open space of the fields. Only by focussing on the copse would this effect cease; only then could you tell how far you had left to walk and how much ground you'd already covered.

"I don't know what I'm saying sometimes. Words seem to come out of my mouth." Leana's voice was higher than it was in the other place, Sam noticed. She spoke like a shy, mildly posh English girl. "It's like I know what I have to say."

"Believe me; I know exactly how you feel."

"I recognise my eyes when I look in the mirror but nothing else." She shook her head. "But it's like I know what to do. I'm not afraid. I feel protected, somehow."

"I was the same."

"Am I dreaming, Robbie?" Leana looked at him eye to eye for the first time since the music class the day before.

Sam shrugged. "I don't think so. Oh, and it's Sam here. Just Sam."

Leana continued to walk. "When I saw you yesterday I recognised you but I knew I couldn't say anything. I'm sorry."

"I didn't know what to say, so don't worry."

"I went back home last night. After I fell asleep. Back to the cottage."

"What cottage?"

They had reached the copse but neither of them fancied sitting on the small frozen-over bench under the boughs. Something unspoken passed between them and they continued to walk on towards the perimetre of the fields.

"My cottage. Where the well is." Leana dropped her eyes and voice. "The witches. Remember?"

"Oh, yeah," nodded Sam. "What happened?"

"After you fell from the window," Leana began, but then her brows knitted and the old fury Sam had seen before, in Scotland, flared up over her features again. For a moment he thought she was going to hit him. "What were you doing that night, anyway? Did you really climb out of the window?"

"I was looking for you!" He pushed it further. "I wouldn't have even gone looking for you if you'd not decided to ignore me. What was I supposed to do? I wanted to speak to you. I thought you'd understand."

Leana wanted to say something but too much had happened. She shook her head, trying to clear it, looked up at the sky and recovered her composure. "Well, you fell from the walls," she began slowly. "I knew nothing of this. A servant came to my room and I went down for you. It was the same night the King was murdered."

"Macbeth did it! I heard them talking about it. Him and his wife!"

"I know, I know," nodded Leana. But then she processed what he was saying and leant forward, her amber eyes wide open.

"Are you sure?"

"Definitely. We're studying the play in English," Sam told her excitedly. "I know everything that's going on. I thought that was why I was dreaming about it, but obviously not. I mean, here you are. But it's all there. We're reading it in class! That night, when I was looking for you, I hit an owl that was in a nook in the wall with my fingers; the owl cried out as it flew out of the hole and that noise was in the play! That was there! But I did it first, do you see? I didn't know it was going to happen. I did it first. That's how I know!"

Leana couldn't take this in. She sank back into her angry state. "I can't believe you thought climbing the castle walls was a good idea."

"Not climbing exactly." Sam grinned, wagging a finger. He'd worked a hole in the sleeve of his jumper as most boy's did, and his thumb poked through it. "Traversing."

"Do you know how dangerous that was? Do you know what I had to do to protect you afterwards? They thought it was you who had murdered the King. Someone had seen a body jumping or falling from the castle. They thought it was the murderer escaping."

Sam stopped, shocked. They were two small dots in the vast blanket of frost. "What did you do?"

"I took you to the cottage."

"Why do you go there if you obviously don't like it? I can see it upsets you. I don't get it."

Leana again grew angry. "Well, where was I supposed to go?"

"I don't know. Anywhere?"

Throwing her hands high above her head, Leana walked away. Sam took off after her, catching her up, smoke billowing from his mouth as he asked, "And what? Is that where I am now?" He tried to make her look at him but she avoided his eyes. "Tell me what happened. You said you were going to tell me what happened."

"That's where I thought *we* were." Leana jabbed him in the chest. "And do you know what? I'm sick of saving you."

"Saving me?" Sam tried to look confused and shocked at the same time, aping the way actors did it in films, arms outstretched, eyebrows raised, but he quickly realised there was no one to see him. Leana had gone. She was walking back towards the Main Building, fast. Sam began to jog after her but within a few strides he gave up.

Cupping his hands to his mouth, he shouted, "I don't know why you have to be so angry all the time!" and heard his voice echo back to him.

Ahhnnngreee all the time-time-time.

That afternoon he *was* like a dog left behind in a house, occasionally kneeling up on the arms of his chair in the common room to peer out through the steamed up windows of St Nick's at the frighteningly empty school.

He watched a film until lunchtime but then ate alone with one older girl, of at least eighteen, in the dining room, from a series of bowls which had been left covered with foil. Apart from "hello" and "goodbye", the girl didn't say a word. She played a game on her phone the whole time and walked out speaking what sounded to Sam's ear like Dutch or German. "Nay, nay, nay..."

He walked back to the house in dim twilight as snow started to fall. He could see it sliding diagonally through the air by the yellow street lamps, which lined the school drive, and instead of making him feel cosy and Christmassy as snow usually did, it made him feel totally and utterly alone. *I am lost in the Arctic desert*, he thought dramatically.

He watched the news and changed chairs. He switched channels every ten seconds, even watching some curling at one point. He doodled on the back of his wrist with a pen.

Finally Pram came back from his day out, startling Sam by

crashing open the common room door and demanding to watch American Football. Sam acquiesced. A new thought had begun to terrify him – that perhaps Leana was so angry with him and so crazy that she might do the other him – Robbie Cauldhame – some damage. Somewhere, in the other world, Robbie was lying in a ramshackle cottage near a poisoned well surrounded by witches which manifested themselves in fog.

"You shouldn't bite your nails," admonished Pram.

"You should use deodorant."

"I use deodorant!" Pram shot back, appending the phrase with a variety of swearwords he'd learned at the school. Sam was amused to see, as he left, that Pram was gingerly sniffing beneath his raised arm.

Sam went to bed. He tried to come up with something to think about. *What do I want to think about before I die?* he thought. But all he could think about was Leana. This he found very depressing. But she did have pretty eyes. She was actually really nice even when she was angry.

Would you think she was lovely even if you knew she was going to kill you?

Yes, I would. I would fancy her even if she was going to kill me.

I like her. This in an indisputable fact.

Sam fell into a feverish sleep, which took in aspects of little red riding hood – *what big teeth you have, dear!* – and some kind of skiing adventure in which he was an ace jumper who broke his leg but came back from the accident better and wiser (thanks, American films!). Sometime in the early dawn, the curtains ghostly grey, he awoke to a hideous scratching sound, like a giant itching its hairy back.

He sat up, noticing Pram in the only other made bed, flat on his back, snoring quietly. Again it came: fingers on a blackboard. His eyes scanned the gloom until his ears led him up to the drawn curtains He stepped out of bed – *ouch! Freezing!* – and padded to the window.

There, between the gap in the curtains, he saw Leana, her face white as a ghost. She was crying. In a moment Sam was outside in his pyjamas and bare feet, standing in a fresh fall of snow, hugging her so closely he could feel her warm heart beating against his ribs.

10

Evil Cannot Exist Without Good

Dense banks of fog rubbed out parts of the buildings and lampposts. Treetops floated in the air. Kerbstones and ghostly hedges guided them back to the locker room door, which squeaked and rattled on its hinges as they dragged it open.

Sam led them both up the grey-lit corridor to Dorm Four and Leana faced away as he changed. The red digits on the wall above Walt's locker said six ten. Leana took the fleece jacket Sam offered her and they borrowed gloves and scarves from drawers of the other cupboards.

"We shouldn't be in the school," Leana whispered, her voice jittery and weak. "I need to talk to you but not in the school. It's not safe."

"We'll go out for a walk if you want?"

"Yes, yes. Anywhere. Just not here. It's not safe."

Back down in the locker room Sam emptied his backpack of books and filled it with all the food he had left in his tuckbox. The booty was three bags of ready-salted crisps, a dented can of lemonade and two Granny Smith's. "All set. Let's go." With their scarves pulled up over their mouths, the couple walked out of the back door into whitening fog.

"Nobody's going to know if we go out today," Sam said, and meant it. He hadn't seen a teacher since Friday evening. Food appeared in the dining hall as if by magic and there were no set times to check in or be seen. "Let's go up to the Gallops. It's a path that goes all the way around the hills. We did it in cross-country. We can keep walking all the way around or come back when we want. It might even be clearer up there."

Leana didn't mind where they went. She was pale, quiet and drawn. "I'm not going to say anything until we get out of the school," she repeated, looking anxiously behind herself as they walked up the paved route which ran alongside St Nick's.

Sam led them briskly across the dark tarmac drive to the main entrance but paused at the perimetre like a caged bird suddenly afraid to fly. Leana coaxed him over the threshold and they stepped officially Out of Bounds. Directly ahead was a stony footpath, which bisected the teacher's cottages and the senior girl's house, and the couple walked up it in silence, hearing the neighs and snorts of the school ponies before they saw their heads emerge from the mist.

Only when they'd surmounted the stile at the end of the path and had begun to traverse the long, damp grass of the field beyond did they talk. And then it was Sam who spoke, apologising for the misunderstandings of the day before. This was all so new and confusing to him, he stammered. He went on, detailing his theories of why he was dreaming of *Macbeth*; of her; of why this might all be happening until Leana turned on him with a look on her face that stopped him in his tracks.

"Sam, please," she begged, her eyes closed. "I need to tell you what happened to me last night. I need you to listen. Just listen."

The night before Leana had gone to bed in the girls' house as usual, she said. She'd been so tired she'd fallen fast asleep in no time at all. Almost immediately she'd found herself back at the cottage in Scotland where the well was, shivering, alongside Sam's body: the body of Robbie Cauldhame. "You were very cold," she told him as they walked uphill into the woods. "Cold like you were dead. That was what woke me up. The feel of you. It was something terrible."

A noise from outside the hut had alerted Leana to the presence of a man standing by the well. "He was a soldier of the King. A handsome man. Smiling. Almost glowing. And he was with a boy, a younger version of himself; the spit of his father. Both of them were just standing there, calling to me."

When she'd gone out, she said, the soldier had told her he'd been sent by his Lord, the Thane of Ross, to inform Leana her presence was requested at a banquet which was to be held at the castle that night. "The man was very courteous and chivalrous. He was almost magical. His way. His bearing. He knew my name and my position and there seemed no reason to doubt him."

"And the boy? How old was he, anyway?"

"Oh, about our age. He was obviously the soldier's son." Leana held her hands together as she tried to remember. "It was like he was glowing from the inside. Happy, perhaps. Content. Otherworldly."

"I'm surprised you trusted them," Sam interrupted, pricked by jealousy. "Everyone's always going on about how you shouldn't speak to strangers. It's not a bad rule."

"You should be glad I did speak to them," Leana replied firmly. "The boy saved your life for one thing."

"How?"

The boy had given Sam, or Robbie, some kind of potion, which had revived him, Leana said. "You began to breathe more easily straight away," Leana explained. "I really thought you were going to wake up right there and then. You didn't, of course, but I knew you were going to be all right. I knew you were going to live."

"Luckily," replied Sam, sulkily. He'd picked up a branch and was swishing it.

The soldier had insisted, Leana went on, that she accompany him and his son to the castle. Leana was told that Sam would sleep for a few more hours but would recover soon enough and that it was safe to leave him alone in the hut. "You were warm," she said. "I knew I could trust them. I don't know how to explain it now but you have to believe me. I wouldn't have left you if I thought you were in danger."

"No. Alone, unconscious. Totally safe, I'm sure."

Leana rolled her eyes.

She'd ridden to the castle with the others, she said, in foul weather. Although she'd been glad to be in a safe place, she'd not had long to think about anything before things had taken a strange turn.

"We were late for the banquet," she remembered. "When we walked in the others were already feasting and had been for some time. I was making my introductions, glad to see my friends again, when I noticed a strange scene. The soldier had walked right to the front of the hall, where the master was sitting with his people and the clan chiefs, and almost immediately Macbeth began acting strangely."

"How?" asked Sam.

"It was as though he'd seen a ghost," Leana replied. They were walking up a damp, steep path. "It was obvious the problem for Macbeth was the soldier who'd come with me. By simply staring at Macbeth the soldier seemed to be able to make him go out of his mind. The other guests were quite perturbed, like me. None of us knew what to make of it."

"Did Macbeth say anything to you or the boy?" Sam asked.

"No, nothing. I left when the Lady began making her excuses; she said the master had been ill. I felt obliged to leave with the soldier and his son, of course. When we were outside again – it was the dead of night, pitch black and freezing cold – the soldier told me not to worry and that I should return to the hut to take care of you. I said goodbye and he and his son disappeared into the night."

"Who were they?" asked Sam.

Leana shrugged. "I can't say for sure. What I do know is that when I got back to the hut I found you there, still asleep, but you were breathing. As soon as I lay down you began dreaming. Your eyelids were moving, flickering, and I knew you would be well. I lay with you and I talked to you. I told you – do you remember?" Leana looked worried, vulnerable in a way Sam hadn't seen since the first time he'd set eyes on her behind the glowing window on the stormy coast. "Do you remember anything I told you?"

Sam shook his head. "When I'm here I don't think I know anything about what goes on there."

Leana was sad but relieved. She had told him how she had been abandoned as a child in that place, left in a well to die, but how the witches and spirits had taken her as one of their own. How she had grown up able to see things other people couldn't see.

"Tell me," Sam said. "If you want. Tell me it all again."

Leana shook her head. "No, no, no. It's nothing important."

Sam gave her a moment. She had turned away and he could tell she was upset. They walked on uphill on the slippery path. When she had controlled herself, Leana asked him, "Do you remember the spirits we saw when we were at the cottage?"

"The women? The faces in the fog? Of course"

"Well, they came back later that night."

"For you?"

"No."

"For me?" Sam looked worried. Dark boughs floated like twigs in the misty soup swirling above them.

"No."

Sam could feel Leana's nervousness now. The girl was trembling and had turned very pale again. "What's wrong? What happened? Did they hurt you?"

"No, no. I was with you. I heard them talking, that's all. Talking to someone outside."

"Who?"

"Macbeth. They were at the well, all of them. The three sisters and their leader. The chief witch. With him. And he looked as mad as he had at the banquet, worse perhaps. He looked ill."

"He knew the witches?"

"I think he was consulting them."

"But how? What did he ask? What did they say?"

"They said he couldn't be killed by anyone born of a woman. That he would never be defeated until Birnam Wood came to his castle. They spoke of the Lord Macduff, too – do you know him?"

"No."

"He's a good man. Another who I think has suffered and will suffer more before this is done."

"Some of this must be in the play," Sam suddenly declared, turning around. "We should go back and see what it says. I've got the book in my locker!"

"Wait. Sam come back."

"But it's all written down! It has to be. I think I remember some of that stuff. The wood. Macduff."

"Wait, Sam. Please. I have two things to tell you and then we'll do whatever you want."

Sam stopped, unsure. "What? Tell me."

Leana drew close to him. "While Macbeth was talking with the witches I saw the soldier who'd come to me earlier in the day, who'd taken me to the castle – the one who'd helped you."

"He was evil too?"

"No, no. He was conjured up by the witches, I think. A vision. He wasn't there in person. They were saying his children would be Kings." Leana was staring into space, trying to remember. "I think the soldier who came to me was a ghost. To help me. To help us. I think Macbeth might have killed him. That would explain why Macbeth was so anxious when he saw the soldier arrive at the banquet. I don't know exactly – I can't recall every detail of what happened. I was worried about you. It was late, cold – I'm just not sure. I was only relieved that you were not going to die."

Sam saw something in Leana's eyes that shocked him. It was like a softening, as though she were showing him some very sensitive part of herself, her soul, perhaps, some part of herself which she usually kept covered. "Let's go back," he said. "Let's go back and read the play. I'm sure we can work out what to do if we read it."

"What play?" Leana flew into a rage, grinding her teeth and throwing her arms out wide. "This is my life, Sam! Why do you keep talking about a play? I'm trying to tell you what happened to me. I'm trying to tell you how I feel! I am not some character on a page! Feel me!" She pushed him hard with both hands and Sam staggered backwards. "And you are not some wizard who can consult a book and know the future! You're a boy, a piece of all this, like me. We are tiny, insignificant pieces in some game of theirs – these spirits, this evil world!"

"No, no, no, Leana, you have to listen to me, I swear! This is all happening in a play. This has been written down." Sam smiled like a madman. "We've been reading this in English. That's why I go there. Why you come here." He walked towards her, wanting to make peace. "What I don't know is exactly how this is all happening but there has to be an explanation; there has to be rules. There always is. We just need to find the answer, that's all. Everything is rational, even things we can't understand yet."

"Nonsense!" shouted Leana. "You're trying to make sense of something you can never understand!"

"There is always sense," Sam replied. It was his father talking.

"Then who was the Queen of the witches?" asked Leana, folding her arms. She was standing in a fencer's pose, one foot pointing forwards, the other perpendicular to her body.

Her posture and the question silenced Sam. "What?"

"The Queen of the witches. She was there last night. I told you. Their leader. I asked you who she is. Do you know?" Leana widened her eyes. "No? Ah, you haven't read that part of the play yet, have you? Haven't got to that scene yet?"

Sam ignored the sarcasm. "Perhaps we have. What's her name?"

"Oh, but you should know."

"Why?"

"Because it's in your beloved play and because she's here too.

You know her."

"Here?" Sam looked about at the ghostly trees. "I know her? What are you on about?"

"Oh, yes. She's here. Here in the school."

"What? Who? Leana, I don't know what you're talking about. You're a nutter!"

"But she's your leader here. You stand for her when she enters the room. You stand to salute her when she enters your great meetings in the mornings."

"Meetings in the mornings? What? Assembly? Who? Mrs Waters?"

"Very good, Sam." Leana nodded gravely.

Sam couldn't fathom all of this. "Who? Hachet? Seriously?"

Leana crossed her arms. "All so very rational, eh?"

11

The Key To The Abyss

Sam and Leana walked back towards the school. Neither had a watch. Neither knew if it was late or early. For the first time Sam wasn't wondering if this was all a dream – now he was *hoping* it was all a dream. "Perhaps we should run away?" he said out loud. Leana didn't reply, so Sam answered himself. "But where would we go?"

"Why are you at this school?" Leana asked suddenly. "Are your parents dead?"

"No!" Sam gave a hollow little laugh. "It's just that my dad's working away at the moment. He's an archaeologist." He waited for her to be impressed but she blew into her hands.

"And your mother?"

Sam looked away. He didn't know what to say. "She's a writer," he mumbled. Usually people, older people especially, asked if he was related to the famous writer just by his name. Leana again looked unimpressed. "She hasn't been well recently. She left home. The police found her in a hotel by the seaside. On the coast. She didn't seem to be able to remember anything." He looked across at Leana. "She's not very well. My father has to work. I have to be here."

"It must be hard. For all of you."

Sam shrugged. "I'm fine." He stared down the road ahead. The fog made it a white tunnel. "What about you?"

"My family?"

"Yes."

Leana shook her head and buried her chin in her scarf. "I don't have one."

Sam thought about her asking if her parents had died, as she had asked him, but decided to avoid a direct question. "Then who brought you up?"

Leana stared him directly in the eyes. "Three sisters," she replied in a manner which said, *No more questions.*

For a long while they walked on in silence.

As they climbed back over the stile and began down the narrow, hedge-hemmed lane towards the school, Leana asked, "What shall we do if we see her today?"

"Who? Waters?"

"Uh-huh."

"Did she see you last night? At the cottage?"

Leana thought back. "No. I don't think so."

"Then we do nothing. We don't let her know that we know anything." Sam loosened his scarf. "Maybe it's all a game, as you say. Maybe we're doomed. Who knows? Until something happens for certain, I think we should just carry on. What else can we do?" He remembered another phrase of his fathers and repeated it: "One foot in front of the other and follow your nose."

Leana smiled at this and held Sam by the elbow. He could feel she was scared, feel her trembling, and this had a strange effect on him. Although he was scared himself, he overcame his fears for her sake. He put on an act. He would be strong because she needed him to be strong.

Leana was thankful: more than anything she was tired. In her mind she was conscious of being with Sam, of how that was what she wanted, even if it was just for a few minutes, even if disaster was just around the corner – or at the bottom of the lane. For these few moments she could be calm and simply *be.*

The ponies watched them walk by; their black eyes and bridles floating in the air.

"Someone's standing at the bottom of the road by the wall," Sam whispered as they drew closer to the crossroads, the school on the other side of the road. They were hemmed in by old stone walls, as old as the village and the church. On one of these was a rusty iron cross that the children sometimes swung for luck: no one knew what it was really for.

"It's too tall to be Waters."

"I can only see a shape."

"It's a person."

"Let's keep walking. It could be someone walking their dog or waiting for a bus."

Sam felt Leana reach for his hand and as they touched palms he felt a strange fizzle of energy pass between them. *This is too real to be a dream,* he thought. When he looked across at her he wanted her to look at him but she was looking ahead, into the gloom, at the spindly figure in a gown and mortar board hat waiting for them at the bottom of the path.

"I think it's a teacher," Leana whispered.

"Yes. I think you're right." Sam could see the outlines of a wrinkled, taught face. He recognised the face of an old master, one he'd seen in the old black and white photos which hung in the Main Building. "I think he used to be a teacher at the school. I'm pretty sure I've seen him before. He's ancient."

Leana had relaxed when she'd realised the figure waiting for them was not Mrs Waters. Now she dropped Sam's hand. "He's waving to us, I think."

"Hello, sir," said Sam as they came face to face. The old master was tall and tired looking but there was goodness in his face and he smiled as he looked down at them, his grey moustache flickering upwards at its edges like twitching wings.

"Out rather early, aren't we?"

"We're practically the only ones left in school, sir, so we thought we'd take advantage of it and get some air."

"I see." The master looked from Sam to Leana. "Well to my old eyes you both look like you could do with a hot drink. I only popped out to post a letter. Mrs Wickett should be brewing up just about now. Care to join me for a cuppa?"

Mr Chipping's rooms were in the old cottage opposite the school.

His living room was warm and cosy, the shelves filled with books, photographs and magazines, and there was a small pug dozing on the mat in front of an electric fire. The air smelled of carbolic soap and dust.

"Thank you kindly, Mrs Wickett," Mr Chipping told his house lady, who'd brought in a tray of tea and toast. "Just here on the table will be fine."

"Thank you," Leana muttered. She and Sam were perched together awkwardly on a small sofa patterned with blue paisley swirls.

"Must be awful having no homes to go to this weekend of all weekends," Mrs Wickett said, standing for a minute with her hands crossed on her apron and looking at Sam and Leana with sad eyes.

Mr Chipping waved a liver-spotted hand. "Thank you, Mrs Wickett. That'll be all for now."

"Thanks for this," smiled Sam, plucking a triangle of toast.

"And did we see anything interesting on our walk this morning?" asked the old master. He sat in a chair and folded one grey leg over the other.

"It was too foggy to see much, sir," Sam began. "We only went up as far as the Gallops and then we turned back. Did we get to the railway tunnel?"

Leana squinted and stirred her tea. "I'm not sure."

"Young lady, you only joined us here a few days ago, didn't you?"

Leana nodded. "That's right, sir."

"Where were you before?"

Leana opened her mouth to answer but no words were forth-coming. She'd learnt to trust her body to answer for her but now there was nothing there. Only the truth. "Home."

"A long way from here, eh?" Mr Chipping leaned forwards and nudged the pug with the tip of his slipper, warning it to be careful its nose didn't dry out. The small bundle of fur immediately sat up, switched positions and settled again. "And you, young man. Are you happy here?"

"I am, sir."

"With Mr Firmin for English Lit this year, aren't you?"

"That's right, sir."

"Which texts are you studying?"

"*Macbeth*, sir," Sam replied, and went on to list the other two books they were supposed to have read.

"Ah, *Macbeth*," repeated Mr Chipping. He stared down at his tea with a wistful look on his face. "I see."

"This cottage is very old, isn't it, sir?" Sam asked. He was thinking about the horseshoe on the wall outside.

"Yes it is. Almost, but not quite, as old as me."

"Did it form part of some stables before, sir?"

"The old monastery stables. That's right." Mr Chipping winked at Mrs Wickett who had popped her head inside the door. "In fact, some people claim to still hear the old horses from time to time, don't they, Mrs Wickett?"

"They do indeed, Mr Chipping."

"Monastery stables, sir?" asked Sam.

"That's right."

"Hasn't always been a school here, then, sir?"

"No, no."

"I heard it was a hospital in the last war."

"That's right." Mr Chipping saw Leana looking at a photograph of a pretty young woman he had over the fireplace. "My wife," he told her.

"She's beautiful," Leana said.

"Can you tell us about the monastery, sir?" asked Sam. He was thinking of the rumours he'd heard about St Nicks being built on a graveyard, in the shape of a cross.

"Well," sighed the old master. "The grounds covered more or less the site of the current school, I believe. The Main Building is where the abbey stood. They had some farmland hereabouts. A mill, I believe, and a small brewing operation. Of course the whole place was destroyed during the dissolution. Became a kind of hospital after that. A retreat, we might say. Most of the monks escaped, though. Place is honeycombed with tunnels. Surprised nothing has fallen down, especially with all the building work they insist on these days." He turned to stare at his shelves. "An old friend of mine wrote a rather interesting volume about all this, actually. Now, if I could only remember the name of it."

"Do the tunnels still exist?" Leana asked.

"Oh, very probably. I mean, they're relatively recent if you take into consideration the long history of this little village." Mr Chipping squeezed his nose. "Our churchyard for example, just up the way, there. You've noticed its shape, I suppose? Round. The walls, I mean."

Sam thought about it. "Yes, I suppose so."

"Well that's a pretty good indication that pagans were here first, you see, my boy. I would hazard a guess that our little church has been a religious site as long as there's been religions to believe in, which means, of course, as long as there have been people to believe. The current church was built on top of the old site but such imposition can't negate the history of what went before, or what it stood for."

"I'd love to read that book if you could find it, sir."

"Talking of books," said Mr Chipping with a grin. "Perhaps I may indulge you both in a story, since you're so interested in the history of the school?"

Seeing his guests nod, Mr Chipping leaned his head back and looked up at the ceiling. His eyes, to Leana and Sam, seemed dissolve, as though the sockets were emptying. "Now one winter's day a long time ago, on a morning not unlike this one, the story goes that there came a steady knocking at the monastery door.

"The monks who were going about their business inside were

surprised to find an old woman standing in the snow – let's call her Sybil, I like that name – and try as they might to entice her in, the strange old lady wanted nothing but to speak to the abbot and refused to leave until she'd done so.

"Well, the abbot was summonsed and only then did old Sybil reveal what she wanted. That was, she told the bemused abbot, to sell him three books she had with her which, she promised, were of very great importance to the future of the monastery. The only condition she laid down was that the abbot may not read the books before he bought them.

"The abbot rejected this strange offer out of hand – he thought the price too high and had no time for magic and superstition. He slammed the door in poor Sybil's face and told her in no uncertain terms to get off his property.

"Thinking that was the end of the matter, it was with some consternation that a short time later the abbot heard his monks declaring they'd just witnessed the old lady setting one of the books alight on the monastery pathway. Indeed, when he looked out, the abbot saw her standing guard over the fire, watching the pages turn to ash. None of the monks quite knew what to make of this sight but they hoped it was the end of the matter.

"But it wasn't.

"Old Sybil returned to the monastery door and knocked again, once again refusing to speak to anyone but the abbot. Again she tried to sell the remaining books – two now, of course – but once again she was refused and again the door was slammed in her face.

"Again the monks watched as old Sybil set another tome alight and waited until it burned to ashes. It was about now that the abbot, watching from within with his brother monks, started to become rather worried. When he came to the door the next time, for the old lady rang again, the abbot agreed to buy the final book for the same price the old woman had originally asked for all three.

"Taking the tome into the abbey, the monks and their abbot prepared to pour over the contents but instead found each page completely blank.

"The old lady was never seen again.

"It was not until many years later, after Henry VIII came to the throne, that the monks then inhabiting the monastery thought it might be a good idea to write down their history. For one reason or another a scribe was given old Sybil's book, empty of course, but it wasn't long before they found that the tome contained very strange powers. Legend says that it quickly became apparent to this lowly scribe, and later all the monks, that whatever was written on the blank pages could somehow affect both the present and the future of the monastery.

"When the dissolution of the monasteries began, the book, along with most of the valuables kept in the monastery, was secreted out via the tunnels I was telling you about earlier. Nobody quite knows what happened next, but there is talk of the monks becoming trapped in the tunnels and of the book being lost somewhere under the school grounds, where some people say it remains to this day."

Leana smiled. "Do you think the book is buried somewhere under the school, Mr Chipping?"

The old master looked back to them, his eyes faded-green again. "Yes, I do. I think it's hidden. Safe. Waiting for the right person to find it."

"The right person?" asked Leana.

"Not everybody has the power to write in the book and have what they write come true," explained Mr Chipping quietly. "Only some." His eyes were very pale. "Many try. Many are called. Few are chosen."

"You seem to know a lot about the book, sir," Sam said.

"Oh, I've seen it," replied the old master, smiling cryptically. "And held it in my hands."

"When?" Leana was wide-eyed.

"During the last war there was a lot of terrible damage done to the school. There is an airfield not far from here, or there used to be. I don't know if you know it? Well, anyway, the enemy took a great deal of effort to put the runways out of action and in one raid some stray bombs fell upon us. Damage was done, as I say, and all of us made great efforts at the time to save what we could find in the rubble.

"I remember one morning as clearly as if it were yesterday. The whole school in line, passing books, photographs and shelving and what not in a great long line out of this enormous hole in the ground. And one of the books that was thrown up by all this chaos was, I believe, the famous book from the monastery. Old Sybil's book."

Sam was perplexed. "But why do you say that, sir?"

"Because of what happened next." Mr Chipping sipped his tea. "The person in charge of storing the books was the Head Girl of the time, who was a very ambitious, rather bossy girl, but very clever with it. At some point that day I believe she realised what that book was, and the power it held. She must have heard the legend – everyone had at that time, perhaps we were rather more naïve, or open to different interpretations of the world – I'm not sure. But she brought it to me and yes, I did hold it in my hands."

"Did you use it?" asked Leana. "Did you write in it?"

"No," answered the master. His face was very serious now, very pale. "I had other concerns. The bombs had caused great loss of life." He sat silent for a long while and the pug at his feet yawned. Neither Sam nor Leana wanted to interrupt him.

Mr Chipping leaned forwards and stared out of the window at the fog. "The personality of an author shines through in the book they are writing whether they like it or not. Sometimes this is quite unconnected with the subject of the book itself. That is why evil can be so attractive and good, sometimes, so repellent."

Leana looked at Sam and shrugged her shoulders. *What's he on about?*

"Where's the book now, sir?" Sam asked. "Do you know?"

Mr Chipping turned to Leana and Sam with a faraway look on his face. "What?"

"I asked if you knew where the book is, sir?"

"Oh." Mr Chipping shook his head slowly, sadly. "All that is behind me." And then he smiled. "Yes. It's all behind me. Ancient history."

Watching the old man lie back in the chair and close his eyes, Leana nudged Sam and whispered, "Let's go."

They stood up and left the sleeping master and his dog and met Mrs Wickett in the hall by door. "Drop off in the middle of the conversation, did he?" she asked, chuckling.

"Yes," Sam nodded. "Thank you very much for the food and drink."

"That's all right, my dears," smiled Mrs Wickett. She opened the front door and the cold air immediately raced in. "Told you the story of the book, did he? I did hear."

"Yes," nodded Leana.

"Goodbye, children," said the housekeeper, and closed over the door.

"Can we stay out of the school for a while?" Leana asked when they were alone again on the cold, foggy path. "Let's go up to the church and see if we can find any secret tunnels."

"Or books," Sam added with a laugh.

"I don't want to go back to the school," Leana repeated, quietly. And then, as if something suddenly occurred to her, she added: "I think she's here for the book, you know."

"Who?"

"The Queen of the witches."

"Mrs Waters?"

Leana nodded. She felt a cold kiss on her neck and shivered. "She's the most powerful of them all, you know. But if she wants that book, it must be even more powerful than she is."

Sam held her close as they began walking uphill. "Let's not

jump to conclusions. Come on."

Neither of them saw the headmistress watching them from the foggy shadows at the main entrance of the school, hellfire smouldering in the black orbs of her eyes.

12

Hell Is Empty And All The Devils Are Here

The warm lights of *The Admiral Benbow* shone through the first flurries of snow as Sam and Leana walked up towards St Catherine's, the village church. Peering through the thick, low, porthole windows they saw Mr Firmin at the bar chatting with Mr Bukowski and Mr Thomas. The pub was an old coach house, its facades restored: a winter's afternoon two hundred years before would hardly have been any different.

The village shop was closed and the road deserted as far as they could see in either direction as they unhooked the latch and passed into the churchyard. A gaggle of elderly women in drooping hats and flowery dresses were standing in the church porch looking out at the snow falling over the grey tombstones. One of them called out, "You'll catch your death of cold if you don't get a move on, children!"

"Hurry up, hurry inside, that's the way," said another as Sam and Leana jogged up to the porch. "Father Brown has been finally persuaded to put the heating on so do scurry inside. It is worth it, I can assure you."

Incense tickled Sam's nostrils and Leana's ear's pricked up at the sounds of Blake's *Songs of Innocence* wheezing from the organ loft as they walked inside a warm St Catherine's. A small, moon-faced priest was walking towards them from the altar. He might have been smiling but it was difficult to tell. His arms were inter-locked inside the sleeves of his cassock. "You're too late for mass, I'm afraid, children."

Sam smiled. "We were wondering if you could tell us a bit about the history of the church, father."

"Ah, I see." The priest tapped his mouth with a white, clean finger. "Righto. Here's what we'll do. You'll give me five short minutes to say goodbye to Miss Julian, Miss Corelli and Mrs McCullers and then I'll see what I can show you. Miss Julian must get back to Norwich and the others want to see her off. Do you think you two can amuse yourselves for a minute while I attend to them?"

"Of course." Sam nodded. He and Leana wandered the aisles separately and Sam was surprised when he turned, later, to see Leana kneeling and praying in front of a stepped bank of votive candles.

"I thought we might start with the crypt," purred the priest's voice, interrupting his thoughts.

"Whatever you think best, father."

They collected Leana and walked up onto the altar where Leana and the priest knelt and crossed themselves. "You'll notice that the chancel is out of alignment with the nave," Father Brown whispered to them, pointing out the discrepancy in the archi-tecture. "This is very common in ancient churches such as ours, with Saxon and Norman heritage. They call it a weeping chancel and we now think the old architects did it on purpose, to try to suggest the inclined head of our Lord as he hung on the cross. See it there?"

Sam, looking back, could see the shoulders of the organist high up in the loft. He was playing Burgess's *Napoleon Symphony*, the great silver pipes, which rose up to the vaulted roof, singing out the story.

"Through this door." Father Brown smiled, extending a hand.

The narrow stairs descended sharply, turning around on themselves like a dog preparing to sleep. They were lit on one side by small bulbs buried somewhere in the brickwork and a cold, rusty handrail slid through their palms as they went circling downwards.

At the bottom of the staircase, Sam was pleasantly surprised to find a dingy but modern room, something like a vaulted brick basement, with a chair, a table, a visitor's book and a huge crucifix hung at the far end. The air was cool, not warm, and Father Brown began pointing out the vaults in the wall. "The work here is wonderful – Flemish. This piece is Bohemian and very typical. And this one here is Percy Mishingan. A most illustrious member of the village – when was it?" He peered over his half-moons to better read the inscription. "1881. Yes, that sounds about right."

Never heard of him, Sam almost said, but a sharp tinkling somewhere near the stairs interrupted him, saving him the embarrassment.

"Father Brown!" came a ringing, echoing call down the stairwell.

"Please excuse me." The priest smiled. "Do feel free to look around."

Leana watched the priest disappear up the stairs and tiptoed across to Sam. "There's nothing here, you know. This is all too modern. The tombs are old but there's no medieval tunnels."

Sam was walking around the floor, reading the worn engravings on the stones under their feet. "I know. But this can't be the only place. There has to be other stuff under here."

After a few minutes more of fruitless searching, Sam and Leana gave up and went back upstairs. Father Brown waved goodbye to them from the doorway of the sacristy and they walked out together into the wintry dusk. "Let's do a loop of the church and go back to the school," Sam suggested. "I'm getting tired. There'll be people coming back now, I hope. I'll stay with you. You won't be on your own."

Leana seemed unsure but they set off two-abreast, walking on either side of a line of old graves, aiming to make a circle of the church. Sam started reading the names on the headstones but the light was bad, the cold was creeping into his bones and he had a strong feeling that there was nothing worth seeing. When he glanced across at Leana he saw the same dispirited look on her face. *You look pretty when you're tired,* he thought, and offered his coat. "Take this."

"You're going to freeze."

"I'm fine."

As Leana let Sam drape his coat over her shoulders she noticed what she thought was a firefly in the deepening shadows beneath some nearby trees. "Look."

Sam followed her arm and saw – his eyes were better than hers – the outline of a man, smoking, leaning on a rake. "I think it's a gardener."

Leana could see him now, too. "Let's keep going. We have to walk past him anyway."

When they got to the corner of the church they both raised a hand in greeting.

"Nice night for it," the gardener called out cryptically. He had a northern accent.

"Yes." Sam turned to Leana and shrugged. "It is, isn't it?"

"Looking for owt in partic'lar?"

"I don't know." Sam shrugged. "Anything interesting?"

"Oh." The gardener pushed the peak of his cap with a dirty thumb. "Well, there's always the lych-gate, if you're after ghouls or ghosts. Old Crace was the last person buried here, not a week past, and he'll be waiting there, of course, to show the new arrivals in." He sniffed and thought. "P'haps you'll find what you're looking for up there, thattaways. That small garden yonder is where the unbaptized children lie, the excommunicated and the suicides. That's where they place the bodies found on the downs, you see; and them that no one claims or wants. There's a fair bit of history there."

Sam stared over at the dark corner they were talking about. "Mind if we have a look?"

"If yer brave enough. Got a life of its own that place."

"Ah, I think we're brave enough," Sam replied, taking Leana's hand. "Thanks a lot."

"Evening to you both," the gardener replied, turning back to his rake.

"If it's the oldest part of the graveyard there might be something," Sam said to Leana as they walked around the mossy graves. "Let's just have a quick look before we go back."

The corner they'd been directed to was separated from the rest of the graveyard by a low but sturdy bramble hedge. There was only one small place to enter where a wooden, mossy trestle arched over the pathway. The gateway wasn't high but Sam and Leana crouched as they walked under it and both were struck by a sudden change as they stepped inside. There was a thickness to the air, a kind of staleness.

"Oh, what a horrible atmosphere this place has," Leana whispered, summing up what both of them were feeling.

"Right, well, nothing here," Sam answered, turning to leave. "Let's go."

"What's that over there?" Leana asked. "Is it a little window?"

Sam turned and saw a small mound in the turf only a few steps ahead. Yes, Leana was right. It looked like there was a small window in the hillock, with a little ledge of turf sticking out over it. "Maybe it's some kind of offering. Something someone's left?"

They moved closer. Sam knelt down, feeling the dampness seep through to his knees. He reached out his finger towards the small pane of glass, rectangular and about the size of a letterbox slot in a door, and tapped it. The glass gave and flapped upwards. "Wow, it's hollow inside, I think," he reported.

Leana had her hands in the pockets of Sam's coat. "Can you reach inside?" When he said he could she quickly added, "But be careful!"

Sam took a deep breath and slid three fingers through the gap. "Nothing," he said. "I think there's more space but I can't feel anything. Should I keep trying?"

Leana shrugged. "Up to you."

Sam reached in until his arm was through the flap up to his elbow. His chin was resting on the wet grass. As he was about to retract his hand his face changed. "Wait. I think I can touch something. It feels metal or wood. It's not soil."

"Maybe a coffin?" Leana wondered quietly.

Sam's eyes widened. "Oh. Didn't think of that."

"Come on, let's go."

"Wait, wait." Sam pulled a face, sucking his bottom lip into his mouth. "There's a handle here. I think it's a handle."

"A handle? Are you sure it's not a bar? For carrying?"

"I'm turning it. Wait, wait, wait." Sam had to use all his strength but suddenly something gave, there was a small explosion of dirt and Sam ended up lying on his back. When they looked back at the mound they saw a large hole in the ground. Sam was first across to look into it.

"Oh, please don't tell me there's someone in there." Leana had her hands to her mouth.

"No," Sam answered, turning to her with a smile on his face. His teeth were spattered with dirt. "Steps!"

The soil steps led them down into dank, fetid darkness but by the time they'd realised how deep they were there seemed to be nothing to do but walk on and on into the cold earth.

The tunnel smelled of worms and soil. Occasionally hanging roots, some sharp, some waspish, would tickle their faces, but Leana pressed herself close to Sam as Sam pressed stubbornly on. *If anything goes wrong I'll just retrace our steps*, he thought. Out loud he said, "We'll just see where it leads. This might be our only chance. It has to be a tunnel!"

For a long time the steps led only downwards but finally there was a levelling out. Sam gingerly felt for the one opening which presented itself – down here, with no fresh air, the empty space before their faces felt as thick as any wall – and they began to move forwards again, shuffling along like children playing trains. After a few minutes of this Leana cried out, "Listen!"

"What?"

"Our feet! Listen to the sound of our feet!"

Sam began to walk forwards again and, sure enough, something had changed. They were walking on stones now, on some kind of soily, cobbled pathway. Both lifted their hands to feel what was above them but the ceiling was earth and it flaked away into their staring, blind eyes and open mouths.

"This has to be one of the old tunnels," Sam whispered. They were alone, in the darkness, walking under the graveyard, and it only seemed right to whisper.

"Do you think it goes right to the school?"

"Dunno. It has to go somewhere."

Although they were both excited at what they were discovering, Sam had noticed something hanging from the ceiling, blocking his way. Thinking the obstruction was a root, they both discovered, after careful examination, a grisly truth: what was hanging from the soil ceiling was a slimy femur, and the remains of an adult's hand. A skeleton, it seemed, had sunk down from one of the graves above.

Despite their best attempts to stay calm, Sam and Leana lost their sense of direction and panicked. They ran headlong into more human remains, crying out to each other as they became separated, clawing at the walls with their blind, bare hands as bones and dirt rained down on them from what seemed like every side.

13

Though Nothing Is Damaged, Everything Is Changed

Sam woke up with a feeling of not being alone. He opened his eyes to white, sterile light and a boy in a bed eating grapes from a paper bag. The boy's goofy mother, whose hair was stringy and greasy, smiled at him from the other side of the bed. "Hello, poppet. Are we awake, then?"

"Where am I?"

"The Berghof."

"The hospital?"

"The one and only."

Sam rolled onto his other side – everything hurt – and stared down at a long, busy ward. Walking up the middle of it was Uncle Quentin, blowing on a small white polystyrene cup of machine coffee.

Sam learned from his uncle that he'd been found lying in a ditch near St Catherine's by a young man walking his boxer dog. There'd been no girl with him. He'd been alone, wet, unconscious and suffering from mild hypothermia.

The police and Uncle Quentin seemed to think he'd been climbing a tree, or perhaps walking along the narrow stone wall of the churchyard, when he'd fallen and banged his head. Sam said he couldn't remember. It seemed easier.

Uncle Quentin lived in a nice house near one of the biggest racecourses in southern England and from Sam's room he could oversee the course. Sam's father stayed in the same room when he was in the country and one entire shelf was filled with the old man's books and papers. On the wall above the small antique writing desk there was a map filled with place names Sam had never heard of: Erech, Ur, Tepe Mussian and Samarra. His father was somewhere there, digging and working.

On his second night at Uncle Quentin's, eating dinner downstairs for the first time, watching the television news, Sam was told that if he was given the all-clear the next day by the doctors, he could possibly go back to school the following Monday. "Wow, that would be great," Sam had replied, meaning it.

His uncle forked a piece of broccoli into his bearded mouth. "Everything all right there, Sammy?"

"All right where, Uncle?"

"At school."

Sam nodded. "Why?"

"Oh, nothing. If you're fine, you're fine."

The news was a report on violence in the Middle East. Knowing Sam's father was somewhere thereabouts, Uncle Quentin changed the channel to a quiz show with loud, bombastic music and machine gun applause.

"Well, you know what? There is something I think we should talk about."

Sam guessed, from the tone, that his uncle had been talking to Mrs Waters.

"I've heard a few reports," Uncle Quentin began, putting down his knife and fork and knitting his fingers. "Nothing serious, but reports nonetheless, that you've been having a few problems concentrating in your classes. Obviously it's not related, but this little incident – yes, I know it was an accident – but this little incident is a bit worrying, I'm afraid, especially if you look at everything together. The school's rather worried, that's for certain. I'm not so sure."

"I've just been having some really weird dreams." Sam said. "Trying to get used to all the rules and things, too."

"What have you been having strange dreams about?"

"Oh, I don't know. Nothing really. Just really vivid ones. Kind of difficult to know if they're real or not. That kind of thing."

"At night, or – or in the day too?"

"I'm not seeing things, Uncle. They're just dreams, that's all."

"Well –" Uncle Quentin went on eating – "It's been a big change in your life, for sure. Lots of changes." A pause. "Do you think you'd like to speak to someone about all of this? Do you think that make things easier? The transition and so on?"

"Talk about what? The dreams?"

"Yes. Everything. About how you're feeling. All the changes. Your mum and dad, maybe?"

Sam thought about it. "No."

Uncle Quentin nodded. "Righto."

There was something about the way he gave Sam one last look, the way he studied him when Sam thought he wasn't looking, that told the boy that his uncle was not going to let the matter drop. It only made Sam more determined to keep everything secret.

He sat up in his room that night feeling very alone.

I'm going mad, he thought. *I'm actually mad. I see things and hear things that I think are real. I have a girlfriend who is not real.*

Girlfriend?

He thought of Leana. Perhaps she was his girlfriend. Now he was very glad he hadn't asked his uncle more about her when he'd been told what had happened to him. Something, some feeling, had stopped him. If he'd mentioned Leana that would have been that: straight to the psychologist and very probably straight into a padded cell.

Leana, it seemed, had gone back to school or to her world. That's the only thing that could have happened. If she was at school, Sam would see her next week. If she was back in her own world, well – Sam glanced at the clock and yawned – perhaps he'd see her tonight?

But in the morning he woke up in his uncle's house and sat up and looked down on a lone rider galloping along one of the snowy straights of the racecourse.

She's at school, he told himself. *She has to be. I just need to get back there and I'll see her.*

After breakfast Sam drove through the slush with his uncle to the hospital and a woman in white shone lights in his eyes, inserted him into a machine and, finally, after a long wait in a busy room, declared him "fighting fit". In the car on the way to a restaurant for lunch, his uncle asked him, apparently breezily, "So? Any dreams last night?"

"Can't remember," answered Sam, honestly. But then he made up a good tale about an army of huge birds which seemed to make Uncle Quentin happy.

"You've got a vivid imagination all right." His uncle chuckled. "Want to know what I dreamed about?"

Sam didn't say anything but his uncle told him anyway. While he was talking, Sam looked out of the window at the people passing by. It all seemed so cluttered here, in town. To his surprise Sam realised that he wanted to go back to the school, to the countryside. He missed his dorm-mates. He missed the routines. He missed the peace of the hills and woods.

And yes, he wanted to see Leana.

When he thought of her it was like the darkness in his mind suddenly lightened.

On his last night at Uncle Quentin's, after dinner, Sam brushed his finger along the spines of the books on his father's shelf. One of them, lime green and old-looking, took his fancy. It said Desk Diary and the date showed it was three years old. Sam opened it, saw it was full of cuttings and notes, and, careful not to drop anything, took it with him to his bed.

There were odd pencil engravings, scratchings and weird symbols in the book but Sam was used to such things: he'd grown up in a house were a tablet on the table would be made of clay not silicon. It felt strange to see his father's writing, though, and to see the almost whole coffee cup stains on some pages. How close was he, but how far?

In the diary he saw that on some days his father had scribbled notes like "Do people know which plants they pass? Which trees they see? What makes the sky? What lies in the soil beneath their feet" and this brought back acute, bittersweet memories of being in a park in sunny weather, on his father's shoulders, having different trees and plants pointed out to him. He felt an old ache inside which he'd been slowly learning to ignore. It was easier here, where no one was looking, to admit that he missed his dad.

Come on, concentrate. Keep reading. Keep yourself busy.

Was that his voice or his father's?

The newspaper stories were clippings about sites and digs and Sam soon decided he didn't want to upset himself anymore by looking through the diary. "Be brave, Sam, be brave," he could hear his father saying and, just as he was about to close the covers, his eyes were drawn to small illustrations of the moon's phases at the bottom of each page of the diary. Staring at these, Sam could feel his own mind trying to tell himself something. He had the feeling that something about the symbols was important; that they were something he needed to know.

And then it hit him:

The Moon. Leana. Him.

Things happen when there's a full moon.

Do they?

Quickly Sam checked the dates for the nights he'd gone to Leana's world but with a sinking feeling he saw that none matched the times of the full moons in the diary. Again, he felt like crying. *I'm trying to make sense of nonsense.*

As he tucked the diary back onto the shelf he took out the next book, *The Dictionary of Gods and Goddesses*. This was well thumbed and Sam had read it many times before – he liked the pictures. *No wonder I'm a nutter and have weird dreams if this is the sort of bedside reading I've had since I was a child*, he thought. But there was pride in the thought, too. Even as a child he'd loved what his parents did, sailing or flying off to far-off places to sift through the sands looking for the past. It had been normal to him. Birthday parties at museums. Private walks and tours of Egyptian treasures. He'd held ancient Roman coins in his own hands, touched Bronze Age weapons.

Turning the pages, lying flat on the bed and yawning, he found himself staring at a beautiful, horned woman with wings and a chariot. His eyes focussed on the page properly and skipped to the text: "In Greek mythology Selene was the Goddess of the Moon," the entry began.

"Selene," Sam repeated aloud.

'Til Selene's eyes blink thrice, he heard again in his mind. Isn't that what the witches had said that night, when they had appeared to he and Leana?

Sam stared at the picture on the page again. What he'd thought were horns was a crescent moon which she wore in her beautiful flowing hair. "Until your eyes blink?" Sam repeated, addressing the goddess. "What does that mean?"

He went back to the diary and checked the dates again for the crescent moon, for the full moon – for any connection between the phases of the moon and the days and nights when he and Leana had journeyed between worlds but there was nothing. No connection.

He wandered back to his bed and stared at the maps and bookshelf and the shadowy corners of the room in something like desperation. *What am I doing wrong?*

Sam brushed his teeth in a state of dejection. But as he switched off the light in the bathroom and wandered back down the landing he noticed his uncle's alarm clock display by the bed. He read the time and, most importantly, the date. And then it struck him. Of course the dates in his father's diary were wrong: the diary was three years old!

He stopped with his hand on the bannisters and looked down to where his uncle was sitting in an armchair watching television. "Uncle? Can I speak to you a sec?"

"Come down, come down."

Sam danced down the stairs.

"What's up, big man?" his uncle asked. "Have I got it too loud?" He picked up the hand-control and began lowering the volume. "That's the trouble with not having neighbours, you see. You start getting indulgent."

"No, it's not the television."

"Bad dreams?" Uncle Quentin looked nervous.

"No, no. It's something. A project I'm doing. For school."

"Ah, just remembered your homework, eh? Now you're going back?"

Sam smiled ruefully. "Yeah."

"What do you need?"

"I need to know when the last full moon was. Actually, I need to know when all the full moons have been and will be this year."

Uncle Quentin picked up his phone. "I can probably get something on this." He stroked his chin. "No. Use my computer. It's there on the table there. All yours."

"Really?" Sam skipped down the last of the stairs. "Thanks so much."

"Go mad," replied his uncle, turning back to the television.

Sam flipped up the lid and fired up the computer. "What's your password, Uncle?" he asked.

"Macbeth," his uncle called back.

Sam stopped dead. He peeped around the screen but the back of his uncle's head remained still. It hadn't been a joke.

"Macbeth," Sam repeated.

"It was your aunt's idea. Some detective she liked on the telly."

Sam forced a dry chuckle. He keyed in the password and started searching.

All the dates matched.
'Til Selene's eyes blink thrice.
She'd blinked twice now, Sam thought.
One blink left.

14

Castles And Air

Leana felt enormous pressure on her chest. She had a mouthful of goo and a clanging, dizzying ache ringing through her head. Somehow she knew that if she didn't move, she'd die. She could see nothing. She was buried.

Move she did, forcing her body to turn from side to side – it was like she was stuck in syrup – until she could use her hands to push the slimy soil packed tightly around her away. Wriggling upwards, Leana felt cold air on her fingertips and managed to force her head out into damp, dirty but fresh air.

There was muck in her eyes, her hands were gloved in stinking mud and she was in some sort of pit. As sweet as it was to breathe, the stinking air made her retch and, pulling herself out of the slime and onto her knees, Leana scoped anxiously around for an escape route. Up above her, in the roof, was a grill. Half-light was leaking through the squares, and what looked like seaweed or entrails were dangling from the ironwork, swinging gently where they hung lowest.

As Leana's eyes adjusted she noticed a series of steps leading up from one corner of the pit not far away from where she was and she forced herself to wade across to the first slippery stone. In her hurry to get out of the sludge, Leana misjudged the smoothness of the step, slipped and tumbled backwards into the pit. Half-swimming, she crawled out again, hauling herself onto the step as a fat rat ran over her knuckles. Using tiny crevices in the wall as handholds, Leana managed to stand and began moving gingerly upwards.

The staircase was narrow and attached to the wall. There was no bannister or handrail on the other side and Leana knew that if she made another wrong move she'd fall again. Halfway up she thought of Sam, calling out to him with both names, but in a kind of scared half-whisper and with no real conviction. She knew she was back in Scotland and not at the school. The smell of the place, the feeling in the air, was completely different here. She hoped Sam was not with her, as lonely as that made her feel. He didn't belong in this place.

Near the top of the staircase she could see a wooden trapdoor near the grate in the roof and she took the air at a tiny archer's slit in the wall. A knife-blade winter wind cut in through the gap and made her eyes water but she could see, out on the beaten, pale green heathland, the flag of the Thane of Ross. His party – her people – were riding away from wherever she was, towards the brow of a hill where the sun was setting.

"Pray don't leave me," she whispered.

At the top of the steps Leana reached and shouldered the trapdoor upwards, doing her best to ignore the slippery stones she was standing on and the long drop to the pit which lay next to her. The wood rose to reveal a straw-strewn cellar floor but no signs of life.

Leana managed to clamber up onto the floor of this room and let the trapdoor softly down behind her. Now she was aware of being in a castle, a room in the Keep she thought, but she couldn't be sure which castle she was in. She hadn't recognised the countryside and didn't recognise the room.

Walking down towards its farthest end, where a spindly torch flickered on the wall in a draught, Leana heard vague cries which she took to be gulls. Unbolting and easing open the main wooden door she saw a staircase and an open window. She was in a tower and, peering out of the open window, she realised the cries she'd heard weren't gulls at all: they were the shrieks of women and children.

Peering down from behind the dirty flapping cloth covering the window Leana witnessed a grim scene of chaos below. Flashing swords turned tunics from white to red. Pigs and goats were squealing, running out of the dwellings pressed up against the inner castle walls which were being systematically set alight.

What devilry is this?

Leana looked up and saw Macduff's standard flying from the castle roof. She knew some great war was raging here in the castle and in the country beyond: she could sense the turbulence in the air and the crazed, murderous rage of the invaders mercilessly slaying whoever crossed their path. The sound of armoured boots clanking up stone steps alerted Leana to imminent danger and she ran upwards, hearing a sickening cry from further below in the stairwell. The shriek of a sword on stone echoed up to her and scared her so much she ran on, hitching up the hems of her sodden skirts, eager to get as high up the tower as she could but not knowing what she was going to do when she got there.

Emerging out onto the narrow, crumbing battlements Leana saw gulls cawing in the blustery air. She ran as far as she could along the curtain wall ahead of her, heading all the time in the general direction of the gatehouse. She came to a break in the walkway and battlements, a damaged gap, which looked too far to jump across, and paused for thought. Down below she could see the steely-grey snake of the moat and smoke from the fires on its furthest bank but an arrow whistling past her ear and snapping against the crenels in front of her reminded her she had no time. One glance back was long enough to see an archer pulling a fresh arrow from his quiver. He was standing at the tower door she'd run out of.

"Halt, lass!" he cried, his black beard cracking open to reveal blacker teeth.

Leana took a step back, steadied herself and leapt into the air with the fiercest spring she could muster. Whilst she was off the ground she heard nothing but the wind. She saw fires below and they were beautiful. She saw a yellow-eyed gull hanging in the air, totally still, alongside her. They were both, for an instant, flying. And then she landed, knees cracking into the stone walkway and she was away – adrenaline numbing the pain – running for the gatehouse again, another arrow whistling past her head.

At the end of the curtain wall was a long drop to the courtyard. The gatehouse was ahead but too far; not connected to the curtain wall. Leana climbed up onto a crenel and hauled herself onto the highest merlon, the setting sun lighting the sky behind the far-off hills – and jumped.

Down below the water of the moat was grey as granite and almost as hard.

Leana came up, spluttering, lungs bursting from the shock of the cold, and swam for the far bank. Thwacks fizzed and she heard thunder under the water but nothing struck her.

Climbing out through the reeds, Leana found herself staring into the face of a gleaming black stallion that whinnied and scratched at the turf. Leana controlled her violent, shuddering breaths. "Come here, bonny lad. Come here. Let's get out of here, you and me. Let's ride away from all this. Ride away."

The stallion examined the girl with black eyes who smelled so strangely. Behind her the fires in the castle lit the sky orange. The stallion lowered its starred nose and came in to nuzzle the girl and Leana pulled herself up onto its strong, broad back and whispered kind words into the beast's ear as she turned him and kicked for freedom.

But almost as soon as she began to gallop she noticed a figure in black standing in the middle of tracks. "Stop in the name of the King!" the man shouted.

Leana was caught in two minds. It was an old man, bald, somewhat wild, but the words – and the authority invested in them and the way the man delivered them – made her draw up the horse.

"Dismount!" cried the man.

Leana did as she was told. The man came across to the horse and Leana could see Macduff's castle, ablaze, behind him.

"I am a doctor," he declared angrily. "My horse has been taken. My possessions stolen. I have been commanded by the King to attend to the Queen immediately." He had one foot in the stirrups but the stallion seemed to have no interest in allowing him to saddle up. The black beast turned first one way and then the other and ignored the doctor's attempts to beat it with his bare hands or force it to submit with the bridle. "Make your beast allow me mount!"

"He's not mine, sir," Leana answered.

The doctor became enraged and threw his balled fists up angrily at the sky. The stallion meanwhile trotted over to Leana and bowed its head.

"Not yours, ye say?" the doctor cried. "Not yours and he acts thus?"

"He's not mine, sir."

The doctor put his hands on his thighs and panted. "I have been ordered to attend to the Queen," he repeated. "Can ye take me to the King's castle? Know ye the way?"

"I do, sir," answered Leana.

"Then prithee, take me. Take me now. There will be a reward for ye in all this."

Leana thought of Sam in the hut. "I will take you, sir, if you promise to do one thing for me," she said. The doctor exploded again with rage and walked in small circles on the grass with his hands balled but finally he gave in and walked over to where she was standing with the horse.

"What?" He was a man of about sixty. Unshaven with long side-whiskers and hair coming out his nose. "What? What? What?"

"You will attend to my husband," Leana told him. "I live near the King's castle. We will rest there for the night and in the morning you will be able to attend to Her Majesty."

"Get me into the saddle and you have a deal," the doctor replied.

Leana bowed. "'Tis done."
She was thinking, *My husband*!

15

On The Eleventh Hour Of The Eleventh Day

Uncle Quentin drove Sam back to St Francis's to drop him off. He parked outside the Main Building, next to a Rolls-Royce in which a fourth-year boy was eating a full roast dinner in the backseat while his parents sat in the front. Sam, who was used to this odd occurrence, had to tell his uncle to stop staring. "They do it every Sunday," Sam explained.

Uncle Quentin helped Sam get his bags out of the boot. "Any repeats of those dreams of yours and you give me a call straight away, all right, big man?"

"Yes, of course."

"Your father'll be home for half-term. Let's not give him anything to worry about, eh?" Quentin winked and climbed into the driver's seat. Sam noticed his uncle trying not to stare into the Rolls as he fumbled with his keys. Sam waited for him to reverse and waved until the grey Peugeot had swung away out of the drive.

"We thought you'd run away with your girlfriend," a female voice declared from behind him. Sam turned to see a tall, thin third-year called Katy Carr with a much smaller, zitty girl he didn't recognise. The tail of Katy's scarf was trailing in the dirty snow at their feet. Behind the girls, beyond a peeling yellow fence, an extractor pipe was pumping out steam from the school kitchens.

"What happened to Leana?" asked Sam, heaving his bag onto his shoulder.

"What happened to *you*?" Katy shot back.

Sam turned towards St Nick's. It was late and he wasn't sure what to say. But he supposed he'd have to say something sometime – and he wanted to know about Leana. "We were out walking and we got lost in the snow. I can't remember much after that."

Katy folded her arms. "That's not what we heard."

"What did you hear?"

"That's for us to know and for you to find out," crowed the little, zitty girl. She was a strange, rat-faced creature with a mouthful of short, stumpy teeth.

"Fine," Sam agreed. "Well, I'm gonna go inside now or I'll get done."

"Leana was running away," Katy sang. "You went to try and get her back and you got into a fight with some gypsies on the path up to the Gallops. We reckon you were running away with her and you're just saying that you went for a walk so you don't get expelled like she did. They found a backpack on you and you'd put food in it and stuff so you'd be able to survive for a few days. The police got the gypsies but they're saying that when they get out they're gonna come back to the school and go for anyone and everyone. You've more or less given everyone a death sentence, Lawrence, so well done."

Sam took a moment to take all of this information in. "Leana was expelled?"

"Hachet did it that Sunday night while you were wasting valuable NHS time. Leana told Hachet you went to get her, to stop her leaving, and she pushed you over the church wall. She was trying to get you out of it but some of the girls in Burmester saw the gypsies in the pony field and then the police got involved and everyone found out the truth. Hatchet told Bainbridge the whole story and Bainbridge told her sister on the phone the other night. That's how we know. Bainbridge is *loud*." Katy smiled and blew up her fringe. "Very brave of you, Lawrence. Made a right mess, you have. Not only are we all going to die but now The Magistrate have stopped all leaving privileges."

Sam shrugged his shoulders. "A man's gotta do what a man's

gotta do," he said.

As he walked away he heard Katy shouting, "I told you he did it!"

Sam headed for the yellow light outside St Nick's and walked in through the boot room door. There was no great welcome home. As he walked into the locker room Renton from Dorm Six, snaffling a bag of crisps and eager not to share them, crushed the pack, spat in it and turned his back.

Steam from the showers drifted out to where boys were lying on the benches swapping stickers and reading magazines. Sam shuffled up past the towel room and at the cross where all the corridor's met he caught the eye of Mr Dahl, pinning something to the notice board. The housemaster nodded and grunted, "Brave but futile, Lawrence."

"Thanks, sir."

"Leave women to their own devices and you'll stay sane."

"Righto. Thanks, sir."

"You'll never understand them, nor they us. Worry about yourself."

"I will, sir."

"Get unpacked, then."

"Yes, sir. Thank you, sir."

Sam dug his hands into his pockets and walked up to his dorm. Orhan had Turkish pop music playing and three of the boys were occupied with a console on Walt's bunk. "Did your uncle give you any dosh?" Orhan asked Sam – the only comment any of them made to show they knew he'd been away.

"No. Why?"

"Burroughs's been made a Junior Praetor," came the answer. All eyes turned to Eddie Burroughs who was on a top bunk with his head resting on the sausage-like thighs of a swimsuit model.

Burroughs winked at Sam and tapped the small white square he'd had sown into the school jumper he was wearing even though it was Sunday night. "Connections, lads. Connections.

It's not what you know, it's who you know."

"He has Prep with Jimmy Hilton," Kap Tagore explained. Hilton was the current Head Boy of the school.

"Buttering him up," Walt Schulberg put in.

Burroughs sniffed. "It worked didn't it?"

"What does it actually mean, though?" asked Sam, unpacking. "You don't have to wear slippers in the house?"

"Village shop whenever he wants," said Orhan.

"Whenever *we* want," corrected Femi.

"For a commission," appended Burroughs.

"Access to The Eleusinian Room and Magistrates Meetings," continued Tagore.

Orhan rubbed his hands. "So finally we'll get to know what goes on in there!"

"Forget that," Burroughs answered, shaking his head. "No way. My life's worth more than that."

"Oh, so you're one of *them* now?" Femi sneered.

"Definitely," nodded Eddie Burroughs. "Better than being one of you losers!"

The conversation was interrupted by Mr Dahl poking his head around the door. "Number One uniform tomorrow, lads. If you haven't got your blazers out of storage, speak to matron now, please. Clean white shirts, and make sure they're pressed. Regulation school ties only, skinny sides tucked in, fat sides out. Polished shoes, brushed hair and a smile on your ugly mugs if you please." His one-eye swivelled around and focussed on the top bunk. "Oh, and, Mr Burroughs?"

"Yes, sir?" asked Eddie, turning pale. He wasn't sure if he'd said anything.

"Congratulations on your promotion."

"Thank you, sir."

"And ignore this shower. They're only jealous."

"Yes, sir. Will do, sir."

Monday was Armistice Day and the winter weather seemed also to have called a truce.

The sky burned blue and cloudless from the moment Sam stepped outside the House to when he walked up to St Catherine's with the rest of the school after breakfast.

Although he didn't know yet exactly what had really happened to Leana, the incident during Exeat seemed to have raised his standing within the school. The general take on things seemed to be much as Katy Carr had told it, which was this:

Leana, a new girl with many issues, not least not having a family, had attempted to run away during treacherously snowy conditions during Exeat. Sam, who had a good heart and sympathised, having coming so close to losing his own mother, had gone after Leana to try to convince her to come back.

Some kind of altercation had taken place on Riley's Way, by the churchyard, possibly involving gypsies, gangs from another school, immigrants or escaped prisoners, and Sam had been knocked unconscious in a violent struggle. Leana had abandoned Sam in his time of need, stolen his rucksack filled with all the tuck he had left in the world, and, after being caught shortly after, had been expelled from St Francis's and would never be seen again.

Sam, for his part, felt quite sure he knew where Leana was and that in twenty days he would see her again. Of course he kept this fact very much to himself. Indeed, now that he thought he knew more or less what was going on with him and Leana, he began acting very 'normally'.

"The break's done Lawrence good," Sam overheard Mr de Queiroz telling Mr Dahl at the church gates.

Sam knew he wasn't supposed to hear that or Mr Dahl's reply: "His uncle's talked some sense into him, it seems. Lad's damned with his mother's imagination but without the talent to go with it."

Sam moved on quickly, blocking everything out but the views.

It was strange to walk back into the churchyard that morning as the bright, austere but happy weather made it seem a completely different place from the last time he'd been there with Leana.

The teachers were lined up on either side of the path and the students were forced to walk up to the church between them. This meant Sam couldn't look properly for the corner of the garden where he and Leana had found the tunnel. He was pleased to see, though, once he was inside the church and bunched up on the pews with the other boys, that the same priest they'd spoken to was standing beside the altar going over something in the order of service with Mr Coetzee, the head of the Church Service's Committee.

As they rose for the first hymn, Sam's eyes alighted on the votive candles where he'd seen Leana praying and he missed her, careful to show nothing outwardly.

I'll be with you soon enough, he thought.

Drifting outside after the service, Sam broke off from his friends and walked around St Catherine's to where he and Leana had spoken to the gardener. There was nobody in the shadowed part of the churchyard but Sam wasn't surprised: the gardener was probably inside or at home. It was a Monday after all.

He strolled over to where they'd found the tunnel but there were no strange mounds in the earth, no trestles or hedges, nothing, in fact, but graves. The tombstones looked old but not ancient. Sam could decipher the names and there were flowers in various stages of decomposition in the small pots upon them. He wandered over to where he was sure the tunnel entrance had been and read the name on the gravestone there. It said:

MATTHEW CHIPPING

Mr Chipping?

Underneath the dates was an epigram:

Fate

The willing leads.
The unwilling
it drags along.

"Sam!" came a cry from beside the church. "What do you want from the shop, mate? Eddie's going in!"

Sam ran back to his friends and loitered with them outside while Burroughs went in.

Instead of heading back via the gate in the wall by *The Admiral Benbow*, the boys from Dorm Four joined a pack of senior girls who were passing by, laughing and joking with them as they all walked down the main road. When they got to the crossroads at the school entrance, Orhan and the others broke off and crossed over to the school. Sam lagged behind as the girls filed past him until he stood alone on the pavement.

He was transfixed by the place where Mr Chipping's house had been: the cottages in the old stables where they'd had tea together with Leana. He was staring at a low, pretty house with net curtains and bright hibiscus plants in hanging pots thinking *this place looks nothing like I remember.* A small plaque on the wall read: Chipping Cottage.

A senior girl tapped him on the shoulder as she passed by. "¿Que pasa, Mr Lawrence? You look like you've seen a ghost."

"Who lives in that cottage, Carmen?" Sam asked. "Mr Chipping?"

The girl pulled a face. "Who?"

"Nothing, no." Sam was quick to hide his confusion. "Who lives here again? It's just a question. Nothing more. This is Chipping Cottage, right?"

"Yes, look. It says so. Mr and Mrs Allende live here. They're still at the church. Want to talk to them about something?"

"Oh, no, no. I know what's going on now." Sam rolled his eyes. "I'm just getting confused. Nothing! That's all right. Forget it. Bye! Thanks, Carmen!"

The Spanish girl shook her head and went on into Burmester. Sam skipped across the road and broke into a jog to catch up with the others. He did his best to clear his head quickly. *What was going on?*

In the dinner queue one of the Year Ten girls playfully moulded his hair into the "cool" style of the school and Sam let her. "Are you going out with anyone?" the girl asked as they filed into the warm dining hall.

16

A Miserable Little Pile Of Secrets

A strange thing happened that Micklemas term: Sam relaxed.

He began to play a real part in the daily life of St Francis's: singing in church, laughing in Assembly and trotting up to Prep of an evening whistling Orhan's tunes. Somewhere in his mind he knew that he had to enjoy the time he had while the world was more or less normal. He knew that when the next full moon came around everything would go topsy-turvy again. This was the lull in the storm; the moment the caped superhero was at home watching a film about someone else saving people for a change.

The weather had turned too: out of the violent storms and impervious mists had come a dry, cold days lit up by empty, ultramarine skies and chilly nights pocked with starfields.

Tuesday mornings first period were the best for Sam, walking out onto the crunchy fields in his football kit, studs fighting to grind their way into the frozen ground while wisps of nights dissipated over the distant hills and trees.

Between his interview with Mrs Waters and the next full moon only one conversation of note occurred in Sam's life and that was with Eddie Burroughs one Wednesday afternoon during Integrated Science.

The two dorm-mates had devised an ingenious way of staying out of the classroom for as long as possible. Under the guise of checking a series of weather stations mounted around the perimetre of the school, Eddie and Sam had spent most of the double period walking from one to the other. While it might have been more time-efficient to have checked them individually, the boys had made the circuit together, chatting as they went.

"What exactly do they do in The Eleusinian Room?" Sam asked that day, as they headed down the long, leafy path behind

St Nicks to the second station.

Burroughs laughed with shock. "I can't tell you that, Sammo!"

"Who's gonna hear you here?" Sam had his hands balled in his pockets but they were still cold. It was a bitter November day. They moved on slowly, neither talking, until Eddie piped up.

"Tell you what." Burroughs stopped and turned. His eyes glanced nervously over Sam's shoulder and he dropped his voice. From where they stood Sam could see Mr Dahl's living room window, dark and still as a stagnant fishpond. "I'll tell you what happens in The Eleusinian Room if you tell me what really happened that Exeat weekend with you and the girl."

"You know what happened!"

"Yeah, right." Burroughs spat on the ground. All the boys had started spitting. The fashion was for a strange kind of mannered spit, rolling the tongue and flobbing a small ball of whiteness from the tip, in an arc, to the floor. "They called two ambulances and the police because you fell off a wall." Eddie shook his head. "Pull the other one, Sam. One of the SP's told me you were covered in dirt when they found you. I'm not stupid. There's a story there."

"Sure about that?"

"What did she do, Sam? Bury you? That's what I heard. It's what's giving you the nightmares and playing with your head."

"If I tell you, you tell me what happens in The Magistrate induction ceremony."

Burroughs took a deep breath. "If you promise to never, ever tell anyone." He balled and raised his fist. "I'll kill you if you say anything, man, I swear. I'll deny and deny it but I'll still kill you."

"Calm down." Sam waved his empty palms. "What about you? Can I trust you to say nothing?"

"Of course." Burroughs kicked the soil. "You can trust me, Sammo. I'm a HQ."

"All right, then."

They shook hands.

"You first," said Eddie.

"Me first," nodded Sam. "Right." There was a pause as, reaching the weather station, they checked the level of the rainwater in the marked tubes and Eddie jotted the results into a notebook. Later they'd transfer it electronically and add it to their file. They both fell silent a moment, nodding to a gardener cutting up a tree trunk with an axe before following the path which traced the perimetre wall and took them towards the fields. When they were both certain they were alone Eddie nudged Sam.

"Come on then."

Sam, hands deep in his pockets, gave a sign. "Well, I was covered in dirt because we'd been in a tunnel." Now it was his turn to feel strange and paranoid. He looked about at the trees nearby as if nervous they could hear him. They were passing through some rough ground at the foot of the tennis courts. The children that smoked came here, ducking down among the shrubs and sharing cigarettes they'd hidden up their sleeves.

"What tunnel?"

"A tunnel we'd found in the graveyard." Sam took the lead as they walked single file through a line of dapple-trunked elms and walked out onto the frosty fields. Some of the ice had melted during the morning but it was hardening again as the temperatures dropped with the sun. "You see, we'd bumped into an old teacher who told us about them. There's tunnels under the school."

Burroughs's face turned serious. "I know about the tunnels."

"Well, we had tea with the teacher. I thought he lived over by Burmester, in the old cottage, but the other day I looked and it was completely different. Maybe I was wrong. It was dead foggy the day we met him. I might have made a mistake. I don't think so but everything was strange, to be honest."

"Wait. Who was the teacher?"

"An old master. Even dressed in the old style, you know. The flat hat and the cape. I'd seen him in the photos they have in the Main Building." Sam stopped and wagged a finger. "That's probably why I'm thinking of The Eleusinian Room, actually, because I was in the Main Building yesterday getting photocopies for Mr Maugham and I was looking at the pictures as I waited. He was in all the black and white ones."

"Name?" demanded Eddie.

"Chipping? Chipper?"

"Chipping." Eddie nodded. "He was Headmaster for a bit." Eddie suddenly frowned. "But I don't think he lives around here, though. He's ancient history. I'm not even sure if he's not dead."

"I don't know. Maybe he was visiting. But we saw him. Leana and I. We were there, having tea with him, and I don't know how it got started but he – this Chipping – was talking about the history of the school and he mentioned that there were tunnels – tunnels that connected the school and the church, things like that. Books. A weird story about an old woman and three books."

"That's right." Eddie had turned pale. Surprised.

"So, that's about it. We went up to the church. The priest showed us some things but we didn't find any tunnels. But then when we went outside and found a part of the graveyard where there was a strange kind of tunnel opening, like a hobbit's house, or something. And we climbed in there."

"You climbed into a grave?"

"It wasn't a grave. It was a tunnel. There was a door. It went down underground. It was a real tunnel, heading somewhere. Under the school, I think." But now Sam remembered the skeletons and stopped. "Well. It went under the graves. That I know." He was about to go on, about how he'd gone back to the graveyard to check after the Armistice Day service when Eddie began laughing. "What?" asked Sam.

"You should write all that down, man!" Eddie cried. "What an imagination!"

"Eh? It's true!"

"It's true, he says," said Eddie. There was something about his manner which was screamingly false. *He's scared*, Sam thought. *He knows I'm telling the truth. Or, he's afraid I'm telling the truth.*

They were at the second station, at the top of the fields where a fence separated the school grounds from woodland. They took their measurements and began walking back. Their route took them across what in summer was the cricket square. From there they walked down to the pavilion and onwards to the Quad. The last station was near the school greenhouse on the open land by the gate to the village.

"So," Sam said as they walked under the trees. "Your turn."

Burroughs scoffed. "I'm not telling you anything if you think I'm going to believe that story!"

"It's not a story!"

"Yeah, right."

In the end, desperate to keep up his end of the bargain, Sam made up a story about Leana pushing him over the church wall and attempting to bury him in a grave which had been dug but left open. This came out of nowhere – perhaps he did have a wonderful imagination after all – but it seemed to placate the other boy.

"That's just evil, man," Burroughs laughed, spitting happily, convinced. "No wonder you didn't want to tell anyone."

Sam allowed Eddie to savour this scenario for a few more minutes until, aware that their time was running out, he again asked him to keep up his end of the bargain.

Eddie was reluctant but he was honest, and when Sam applied some pressure, he came shoulder to shoulder with Sam and said, "I'm not going to tell you exactly what they do because if you repeat it people will know that you know."

"Right," nodded Sam. Now it was his turn to be confused.

"But I will tell you something I heard off my brother which turned out to be true. It's something that for some reason people know, so if you repeat it the whole thing can't be traced back to me – know what I mean?"

"Just tell me." Sam smiled, anxiously spotting the last weather station.

"Have you ever been in there? The Eleusinian Room?"

"Maybe. When we were shown around."

"What can you remember?"

"Does it have a kind of high ceiling?"

"It does. Anything else?"

Sam was squinting, trying to recall the interior. But that day was almost impossible to remember clearly. They might have been shown around the school by Mrs Waters, Sam thought, but he could only remember cloudy images. They'd seen two or three schools in the same day, all of them jet-lagged, his mother and father hardly speaking. The Eleusinian Room might have been a dark, panelled room he remembered with a high ceiling filled with bookshelves and some faraway wine-green stained-glass windows. But that might just have well have been in another school altogether. "Tell me. I can't really remember."

"Well, it's a normal room on one side, with panels and stuff," Eddie began, "but then you can go up some hanging stairs and get up to the old library bit. Surely you remember that, with loads and loads of bookshelves going up to a kind of turret? That's the castle window you can see when you're driving in the main gates. When you're inside, you look up and you can see the turret with all the books going around and around. There's a staircase in the middle, also going around, and they can pull up the ladder so you can't get up to the books on the top shelves. It's all in a kind of steel cage, don't you remember?

"There are green windows at the top, right?"

"Yes, like church windows. That's it."

"I remember the windows. I can't remember the books."

"Well, that's it really." Eddie nodded, sniffed and trotted off. "Better get a move on."

Sam chased after him. "That's it?"

"What?"

"You can't just tell me that!"

"But what else do you want to know?"

"I don't know. The ceremony, maybe?"

Eddie pushed out his lip. "Nothing really. All The Magistrate are there. You have your name called and you have to write in The Book and that's it."

"The Book? What book?"

"The Book. The School Book. The famous one. It's nothing."

"What famous one? What are you talking about?"

"The one they tell all the stories about. The one Chips told you about, probably. Well, it's not that one, the original. Nobody knows where the original is – but they have the book up there, on a kind of altar, I suppose. There are two little jars, little urns on each side. They hold the ashes of the other two books, the ones they burned. They're supposedly the real ashes but who knows? They call the big one The Book but it's just a big old ledger type thing, like a big rectangle, with blank pages. All the ones they've already filled out are on a shelf behind, and that's it. You go up, you look for your name and you write something in the book. Like a promise, or a wish."

"What did you write?"

"I'm not going to tell you!"

"But, is it supposed to come true, or what?"

Eddie looked to see if Sam was serious. "I don't know." He bit his fingernails. "That's what they say, isn't it? That some chosen ones can write in it and what they say comes true. That's supposedly why we're all here. But I can't see how. I mean, I can't see how anything like that can come true. It's just magic, isn't it? Or superstition, or whatever." He sniffed. "They say they're trying to find someone who the book listens to. You know what I mean? That what they write comes true. The sword in the stone or something like that, I don't know. It's a nice story."

"Where's the original book, then?"

"I don't know!"

"But do you think it's in the room?"

"Sam, man, you're crazy! It's just a ritual, you know. A ceremony. You're reading too much into it." Eddie spat again. "All the badges and stuff, all that ceremony, it just means I can go to the shop for you lot, that's all. Go out at the weekends. Walk in the front door or wear shoes in the house or whatever. They keep it all secret and make it hard to get into but in the end it's just a game, you know. You have to play the game."

Sam raised an eyebrow. "Sounds like they take it a bit more seriously than a game."

"I think it's all like a copy of religion," Eddie whispered. "They want to make you think of the bible or something, talking about books and words. It's like when they make you swear on a bible in court, you know, to tell the truth. That type of thing."

"So you don't believe in it all?"

Eddie thought about it. "No. Not really."

"But you still wrote in The Book?"

Eddie stopped and stared at Sam. "Did you like that packet of crisps you ate last night, Sammo? The ones I got for you?"

Sam laughed. "Yep. Yummy."

"A-ha," Eddie replied, nodding. The boys stopped to take their last measurements. "Just checking."

17

The Queen And I

"And this man is your husband, ye say?" the doctor asked, kneeling beside the prone body of Robbie Cauldhame.

"That's right, sir," replied Leana. She was watching the broth she had cooking over the fire. She and the doctor had been on the road all night and both were exhausted. They would have a small meal, the soup and some bread they'd bought along the way, and they would sleep. The stone cottage was warming up with the flames. Leana poured them both small beer from a canteen and handed out the mugs. "How do you find him?"

"He breathes. He's alive all right. But he does not wake." The doctor bent over, to listen to Robbie's chest. "I'd say he is well. Sleeping. He looks well. What happened to him?"

"The war."

"He must eat. And drink."

"He will." Leana nodded, ladling out the broth. The doctor took his thankfully. "I have put this bowl for him. When it cools, you'll see. He will eat and drink but he will not wake." She mentioned one of the nurses from the army who'd been coming daily to give him food and drink.

The doctor rubbed his eyes. "Well, lassie, I've lived too long to say this surprises me. Nothing surprises me anymore, in fact." He sipped the soup and nodded his approval. "This is your home, is it, miss?"

"It was. Once." Leana stared around the dank walls. "I come here from time to time."

They ate and drank in a companionable silence. The dark eyeballs of hungry mice flickered in the corners as their twitching noses followed the trails of falling breadcrumbs.

The doctor asked, "You say the King's castle is near?"

"Five miles as the crow flies."

"Then shall we leave at dawn?"

"As you wish."

Leana watched the doctor settle himself for bed and cut her hair in the small glass she had hanging on the wall near the fireplace. She had decided it would be best to go to the King's castle in disguise the next day. The last time she'd been was as part of the Thane of Ross's entourage and although she doubted she'd been noticed, she didn't want to risk being recognised. Within a few moments the doctor was snoring.

What shall we do with our reward, Robbie? Leana thought, looking across at her 'husband'. Where was he? Where was Sam? What would Sam say if he'd heard her calling him her husband? Oh, the idea made her cringe even though no one was watching – but then she smiled. *Oh, but what shall we do with our reward?* she thought again, walking over to feed the gently breathing body the cool broth. As usual he swallowed. He also took beer.

Leana thought she wouldn't sleep but had underestimated how tired she was.

The last thing she heard were the bats.

Macbeth's castle struck Leana as gloomy and forlorn despite standing proudly before a backdrop of gorgeous, snow-drenched Bens. After riding through the dense confines of Birnam Wood, the wide-open heathland was uplifting. Hares sprung out of the path of the black stallion as the sun glittered off a diamond-flashing loch lying low to their right.

There were the usual beggars and invalids gathered around the gatehouse, as well as revellers and peddlers carrying their wares on their backs jostling to be let inside to trade. A smiling sergeant was looking for recruits for the King's Army, offering bed and board, shouting about the opportunities fighting might provide. Beer stalls and meat-roasters were doing a good trade and there was a small cattle market underway in a nearby field, the grass churned up by carts and hoofs.

The aggressive soldiers at the main gate backed down as the doctor revealed his name and reason for their visit. He introduced Leana as one of his staff. As they waited in line to be let into the castle Leana remembered how Sam had said he was reading about Macbeth at school and thought it would be wonderful if he was somehow there, watching all that was happening, like God in the sky. *Life is like a dream*, she thought. *Are you there, Sam? Can you hear me? Are you looking at me from one of those awful old classrooms in the Quad?*

When, almost at midday, she and the doctor were finally admitted to the castle, Leana's attention focussed on the shabbiness and dreariness of the grim sights they found inside. Emaciated donkeys hee-hawed sadly from where they were tethered to iron loops in the walls: their teeth were enormous, their eyes dry, their ribs showing through their worn out hides. Passing by a small anteroom with a dirty rag for a door, Leana spied a group of men drinking and playing dice. They looked like demons gathered around a fire.

There were shrivelled, mummifying heads on poles along the sides of the walled-in, fortified courtyard and a scabby bear stalked back and forth in a rusting cage on an otherwise empty platform. Hunched over women were elbow deep in a wooden tub whose grey, acrid water sloshed down to where a group of half-naked children paddled in the overspill on the slimy cobbles.

The Great Hall where Leana had come with King Malcolm and the Thane of Ross was a shadow of its former self. Hunched over figures were eating somewhere in the darkness, near the remains of the great fireplace, but no torches hung from the walls and no logs spat and flared in the grate. There were no shields, colours, paintings or standards on the walls: no decoration at all to light up the gloomy interior.

Leana could hear some kind of far-off screaming which came and went with the lowing of the cattle. This sound, she realised, the hairs on the back of her neck standing up, was coming from the dungeons.

They were assigned to a room on the second floor which had a fire burning and fresh straw in the mattresses. The first night Leana stayed alone in the room as the doctor attended to the Queen. She took supper there and passed her time drawing or staring out of the windows at the countryside. The doctor, who returned to bed sometime in the very early morning, told her, "Nothing happened this night. Tomorrow you will come with me."

"Very well."

"You may leave the room during the day but not the castle."

"Very well."

"I will sleep."

Later that morning, stepping out into the cold, fresh air on the high walls where the breeze was blustery, Leana took in a calmer scene than the night before. Perhaps the menfolk were out, or asleep, but the castle grounds were busy and calm. Some peddlers had been allowed in and a market set up and despite the armed guards passing about the stalls, Leana felt it secure enough to risk a visit.

She spent a pleasant few hours browsing the shops and stands and watching juggling and minstrel shows. The fools and jesters were funny even if their uniforms were dirty. After a lunch of salted herrings and bread dipped in bad wine, she watched a half-decent avian demonstration with sad-looking kestrels and falcons. The high point was when a hawk escaped its keeper and flew away over the battlements.

Later, when the market was packing up and emptying, Leana noticed the beginning of the feeling she'd sensed the night before creeping back. Fires were being lit by nastily laughing men. The bear had been wheeled out and was being needled: it was growling and snapping, long trails of white goo dangling from its maw. She saw the clowns from earlier in the day swigging from bottles, passing coins. Something bad was coming with the night, Leana felt.

She hurried upstairs and was pleased to find the doctor awake. They took a light supper – the doctor advised her against eating too much, given that they might be awake most of the night – and they left soon after for the Royal Apartments accompanied by a guard.

They passed through raised swords and axes and alongside many bowed heads until a final, liveried servant declared, "Her Majesty's private apartments" and opened a creaking door.

Leana, the doctor and the Queen's chambermaid, who had been waiting for them on the final landing, stepped into a warm, strange-smelling darkness. The chambermaid was a haggard-looking young woman with trembling lips and wet eyes. As they walked inside the room she hung back behind Leana and the doctor, hands fumbling nervously in the front pocket of her apron.

Leana could make out a few objects in the dark: curves of gilded furniture, the edges of the windows and battered shields hanging from the walls. She thought she heard a hissing and looked up at the rafters, at smoke swirling up to some sort of ventilation hole, and fancied she saw, just for an instant, the snakish form of a witch, watching and widening its eyes. In a blink the vision vanished. Perhaps it had never existed at all.

"Here she comes!" hissed the Queen's chambermaid. They all saw a ghostly opening in the darkness, a doorway, and a shadow fill the rectangular space. Lady Macbeth, face lit by candlelight, came gliding through it.

Leana watched the Queen drift into the room and was shocked. The last time she'd seen her, Lady Macbeth had been a proud, awe-inspiring specimen but this creature was a sunken, broken forgery of that original. This was a tortured soul with black eyes, holding a peasant's candle, speaking as though drunk or mad.

She's sleepwalking, Leana thought. *She looks pitiful!*

"This disease is beyond my practice," the doctor whispered.

Leana felt great compassion for the poor Queen.

"Banquo's buried," Lady Macbeth was saying. "He cannot come out on's grave." As she spoke Leana felt a growing sadness at the lady's plight. No wonder things were so wrong. No wonder the castle and the country were in such a mess. It felt wrong to see anyone like this, let alone the Queen.

Stopping suddenly, Lady Macbeth seemed to think she'd heard a knocking and turned to the door with innocent eyes, looking like the young girl she must once have been, before peering into the corners of the room as if for help. Then the same blank gaze alighted directly on Leana and the Queen held out her hand and said, "Come, come, come, come, give me your hand."

Although the doctor tried to hold her back, Leana lifted her arm. The Queen's touch was freezing cold, like a chilled corpse.

"What's done cannot be undone," the Queen was saying, leading Leana from the chamber. The doctor and chambermaid looked on, wide-eyed but helpless. "To bed, to bed, to bed."

Leana let Lady Macbeth lead her through into the Queen's personal bedchamber. The doctor watched in horror as the door was bolted and sealed.

18

An Acausal Connecting Principle

Sam woke up with odd, staccato phrases running through his mind; things that people had said in his dreams and that he felt he had to remember. His dream had been vivid and strange and there had been no obvious explanation for it. The most vivid scenes replayed in his mind as he changed and that made him think that what he had dreamt about was important and that he needed to remember it and that it meant something. But what?

During the cold morning run and a dull breakfast – the porridge was particularly stodgy – Sam found it hard to properly focus on what he was doing. He felt as if one part of him were still dreaming; still in bed. In Assembly he jolted awake when Mrs Waters read out the name of the Indonesian boy he'd spent Exeat with, who happened to be sitting next to him. "What did you do?" Sam whispered to Pram, when the focus of the school's attention had moved elsewhere.

"Ping Pong," answered Pram. When Sam pulled a questioning face, Pram clarified, "In the library."

"Ah."

Sam and Pram went their separate ways at the door of the Assembly Hall but the acts of one that day were to have an effect on the life of the other. While a thick-headed Sam went back to the house and got his books, Pramoedya Mohamed took his place with the other naughty boys and girls outside Mrs Water's office. There were three more condemned persons there that morning and all turned their backs in shame as the junior girls came down the stairs in coats and scarves.

Pram entered the Headmistress's office hoping for the best but fearing the worst. He came out steaming with a sense of sincere injustice. Mrs Waters had threatened to call Pram's parents in Manila and ask them to talk to their son in person, something that Pram thought excessive. In reality, of course, Pram was afraid of his father's reaction: how many times had he told him that the family were sacrificing everything so that Pram could have a better education? So that he could learn English and have a better start in the world than either his father or mother could have ever have imagined?

If anything Pram's anger had only increased by the time he entered the stuffy confines of Room Fourteen for a dose of double English. Confined there, he became overwhelmed with a desire for revenge. He felt like a surfer teetering on the edge of the board, the wave toppling over him. In the class he was invisible – the others ignored him – and sitting at a desk in the second row, near the window, thus ignored by all, he took out a small knife he kept in the band of his Y-fronts and scratched out H-A-C-H-E-T in the desk. He was about to start on the next word – something vulgar – when there was a knock at the window directly above him.

Pram's blood ran cold. It was Mr Wilde, looking down haughtily from atop his long white nose. He raised and waggled a bony, much-ringed finger. The children in the classroom fell silent.

Pram, knowing what was coming, stood up and walked out

He was never seen at St Francis de Sales again.

At exactly the same time as this was happening, Sam was running out of the locker room of St Nicholas House. The combination on his lock hadn't worked and Mr Dahl had had to come and clip it off with a pair of elongated plyers. He was late and his locker was open to anyone who might want to look in it but he had his books and his bag and he was on the way.

It was bitterly cold that morning but Sam wore only a green scarf over his uniform: none of the boys wore coats unless it rained. His hair was growing, thick and forward combed, and he had a look about him, a confidence that he hadn't had before. The bell for the start of classes rang as he jogged up the Quad steps with one hand in his pocket to arrive at Room Fourteen just before Mr Firmin.

The teacher made a grand show of bowing for Sam and ushering him into the warmth. "You first, my good man." The students settled at the sight of the teacher. Sam took a place near the window and was quickly informed of what had happened with Pram a few minutes earlier.

"He's gonna be kicked out for sure," Sam whispered back. "What was he thinking?"

The class began, Firmin handing out homework. Sam had scored well in his essay, which had been a story about how it must have been to be a person living in medieval Scotland at the time of the events in *Macbeth*. "All your own work, Lawrence?" Mr Firmin had asked, moustache bristling, as he'd slapped down the papers.

"Yes, sir. Of course, sir."

"Well, then, very good. Got a bright future ahead of you if you keep writing like that."

"Thank you, sir," said Sam, reddening.

"Your mother would be proud."

"Thank you, sir."

As the class went on Sam looked down at the desk. Pram's last piece of handiwork was glaringly clear among all the biro drawings and old graffiti. There were still splinters sticking out of the edges of letters and the letters themselves had been so deeply and violently carved that Sam could detect the anger the other boy must have felt as he'd done it – and he sympathised. Waters could get you like that.

Mr Firmin's voice droned on and the wall heater sent up a steady stream of heady, warm air. The letters on the desk began to move in a very slow circle. Sam enjoyed the effect, half closing his eyes and letting his eyeballs roll backwards in their sockets. It was a lovely feeling, like having your back tickled or your feet rubbed.

"And who is the Queen of the Witches?" asked Mr Firmin.

"Hecate," answered a boy's voice.

"Hecate," Sam repeated, seeing the word lined up in the desk before him, as though Pram had carved it there.

"Good, good," stated Mr Firmin, moving on.

But Sam had blinked his sleepiness away. The letters had realigned themselves. Now they read HACHET again.

Waters is Hecate, Sam thought. He remembered Leana's words.

Waters is Hecate, he knew.

19

Is A Dream A Lie If It Doesn't Come True Or Is It Something Worse?

"Hold my hand."

"I can't see you. Where are you?"

"Over here. Open the shutters, my child. Push them open and you'll see me."

Leana crept across to the grey outlines of the windows and worked the mechanism. Outside she saw the hanging eye of a waning gibbous moon. Grey cloud floated out on either side of the disc like shredded wings.

"Turn, my child." The Queen's eyes sparkled like moonlit water at the bottom of a well. "Come to me. Hold my hand, my sweet little girl."

Leana came and sat on the edge of the bed. She could hear bats chirping.

"We had a daughter once, you know. A very long time ago it must have been. The poor mite was very ill, you see, and they took her away. She had to be taken away. She was very ill." The Queen was stroking Leana's hands with hard, bony fingers. "Are you her?"

"I think not, ma'am."

"But they say you are an orphan, girl?"

"I lost my family to the sea, ma'am, that is correct."

"You have no family, my dear. Perhaps you are my daughter?"

"Perhaps." Leana hadn't known what to say. She felt sorry for this woman. And, having never known her real mother, some part of her wanted all this to be true. That she was a princess. That this proud but broken woman was her mother. She craved and missed her mother even though she'd never met her.

Lady Macbeth began to sob quietly. She leaned her head

against Leana's shoulder. Her hair, which tickled Leana's face, was hard, prickly and dry. The tears, as they rolled off the Queen's cheeks, burned.

Leana stared up at an oval mirror on the wall behind the bed. It had a brass frame which gave a convex reflection of the scene. She stared into the mirror and wondered, as usual, if she were really present in her life. Who was that girl she could see?

Tattered clouds had come in to cover the moon. The entire chamber was cast into a faded-blue half-light. Leana was thinking, *A Queen is a person. We are only people. I must be nice to her. I must pity her as a mother. As a person. She may be my mother. What did the old lady in the cave tell me years ago? Everyone is your brother and sister – everyone your mother and father. You are never alone.*

"Ye bring her comfort," a deep male voice said.

Leana saw the King standing in the open doorway. His boots and tunic were spattered with wet earth which Leana could smell.

Macbeth looked ill, crooked of spine. He was peering at her from behind a dark, unkempt beard which covered almost all of his face. His hair was long and tousled, twirled in places. Loose, frayed strands swung about his drooping shoulders as he stumbled forwards into the room. The door closed behind him as if by magic.

"Your Majesty." Leana stood and curtseyed. "Are you hurt, sire?"

"Sit, maid, sit," answered the King, waving an arm which seemed to turn the wrong way at the elbow. Leana watched as Macbeth lowered himself into a wooden chair and swigged from a dark bottle he was holding. He sat with his thighs apart and his head lolled to one side, kicking off his filthy boots. "She sleeps?"

"That she does, sire."

"And she thinks ye our daughter?"

"That she does, sire."

"You know, I've seen this before. This thing she does. This unquietness." The King pointed the bottle at Leana. "After she lost ye, or whoever it was – I mean whoever it was wouldnae matter, it just mattered that she lost someone – our child – what matters was that every night I would wake to find her at the foot of the bed searching the floorboards. Every night for a year after we lost ye." He smiled in a horrible way, like a shark. "She would have nae recollection in the morning, though, ye see. Of ye or the search."

Leana listened to guffaws and smashing bottles from outside. "I'm glad to be of some comfort to Your Majesties."

"Who are ye, girl?" asked Macbeth, narrowing his eyes. "I've seen ye before."

"A doctor's servant, Your Majesty. Nothing more."

"Not this time. No, no. Ye've been here before. And on what business?"

Leana was worried the King had remembered her from the night of the banquet. "No, Your Majesty. I've not been here before."

"Ye have the mark of the darkness upon you." Macbeth began to laugh. It was slow at first, quiet and not unhappy. But as he saw the change in Leana at his words Macbeth leaned his head back and roared with laughter. His eyes were wet when he finished. "Ha! 'Tis true! Ye, too, know them, do ye not? And ye, too, have listened too much – thought too much upon their words!"

"They know of things we cannot understand," Leana answered. She knew the King was talking of the witches.

"Aye, right. Things we should not know of," Macbeth replied bitterly, assenting. He drank long and sat silently fuming. "If our Queen's not your mother, lass, who is?"

"Nobody, sir. My mother is dead, sir."

"Ye have no family?"

"I say and know this to be true, sire."

"How did they perish?"

"Swallowed by the sea, sir."

"And ye survived?"

"By God's great mercy, sir."

Macbeth seemed unsure. "Who told ye this story? Remember ye all that happened?"

"My guardians, sir. I was too young to remember."

"Your guardians?"

"Aye, sir." Leana found she couldn't lie. "Three sisters."

Macbeth thought for a long minute, staring at Leana, his lips moving as he procrastinated upon her answers. His eyes widened slowly. "Be ye of woman born, maid?" he asked finally, quietly, almost growling. Leana thought him aggressive and confused. His face paled. "Answer! Be ye of woman born?"

"Of course, sire," was all Leana could think of to answer.

"Prove it."

"Sir! I don't know...how..."

The King stood and dropped the bottle, which shattered. The Queen remained snoring. Without turning, Macbeth banged on the door behind him with both balled fists.

"I mean you no harm, sire."

"Silence, devil!"

Leana remained very still. "Your Majesty. I had a family!" she pleaded, becoming emotional at the memories. She was afraid of the look in Macbeth's eye.

The door opened. Some kind of giant, wearing an executioner's hood, filled the doorway. Its arms were bulky and muscled: filthy with scars and dirt.

"Put her to death," Macbeth told the giant, pushing past him.

"Yes, Your Majesty," nodded the beast.

As soon as his master had left, the giant closed the door and walked into the room towards Leana.

20

What You Seek Is Seeking You

Snow was falling from a slate-grey sky as the children walked past the Main Building and up to the Quad for double geography.

Most filed into their warm rooms as the nine o'clock bell rang but Sam and his classmates remained outside, shivering, until the petite, smiling figure of Mr Yogananda came bounding up the steps ten minutes later waving his hands in apology. His car had slipped off the road that morning, he explained, but there was no damage done.

"Lawrence! Sam Lawrence, my boy. Take this sheet to the staff room and make twenty-two copies, will you? As quick as you like, lad. Thank you, thank you!"

Holding the paper in his numb fingers, Sam went straight back out into the cold. Despite the weather it was always good to be let out of class, for whatever reason. It was like being freed. *Is every snowflake really different?* he wondered, as he walked through the growing flurries. *How can we know that for sure? How can people say that as a fact?*

The Main Building was gorgeously warm but Sam avoided the hall for fear of crossing Mrs Waters on the stairs. He waited patiently outside the staffroom, as he knew he was supposed to – knocking was forbidden – and when a teacher finally appeared, going in, not coming out, Sam asked them for his copies.

Waiting, he looked down the corridor. There was only one other room here: The Eleusinian Room, headquarters of The Magistrate. As he stared at the closed door, Sam thought, *now that would be a wonderful place to hide something like Mr Chipping's secret book. Or a tunnel entrance!* He remembered, too, his conversation with Eddie Burroughs during their weather station walk.

At that instant the door of The Eleusinian Room opened and a swarthy, bald, puffing man in dirty white overalls squeezed out. Sam pretended to be reading the notices pinned behind the glass panels outside the staff room but he could watch what was going on in the reflection in their glass. The cleaner dragged a trolley out of the room and locked the door three times. The old trolley wheels squeaked as the man passed by and Sam concentrated hard on the girl's first-eleven hockey report.

"Here you go, Lawrence. For Mr Yogananda are they, you said?"

"Yes, sir."

"Heard he had a spot of bother with the weather this morning?"

"He did, sir, but he says it's fine now."

"Very good. Off you go then."

"Thank you, sir."

Sam didn't notice the snow as he walked up to the Quad. By the time he was back in the geography room with Mr Yogananda he'd formulated a plan for how he might get into The Eleusinian Room and have a little look about. It would take a spot of planning and some good luck but it was feasible.

After geography came English – they had to draw and label a replica of the Globe Theatre in preparation for a school trip to London in the New Year – but then came break-time. Sam ran ahead of the others to St Nick's and dumped his books and bag in his locker. The dorms were out of bounds but the common room and matron's room were both busy.

Sam pushed through the huddle of queuing, sickly children clogging the corridor outside the matron's room and, his eyes on matron the whole time (she was working opposite, overwhelmed with snivelling patients), tried the handle of the small storeroom he was leaning against. It gave and Sam slipped inside and grabbed what he needed. He repeated the procedure to get out, locking eyes with matron right as the door clicked back into place.

"Away from that bloomin' door, Lawrence, you pest! We've already had to replace the hinges twice and Mr Dahl will have your guts for garters if your leaning on it means he has to do it again."

"Yes, miss, sorry, miss."

Sam walked back down towards the locker room with his booty hidden under his arm.

He spent the rest of the day waiting for lights out. For the first time in many months he thought, *I really want to wake up here tomorrow.*

And he did.

Sam had never been so happy to hear that clanging bell or get up and hop about on the chilly floor. He fairly danced through the snowy morning run and had to control himself when Walt and Femi asked what was up with him. He found it difficult to act normal during assembly but forced himself to listen and participate in the dirge-like hymns.

Back in the locker room at St Nick's he suffered a heart-stopping moment as the rumour went around that classes were going to be cancelled because of the snow. "The roofs'll cave in, they're so badly made," snotty Mark Smith assured them. But finally groups of boys began drifting up towards the Quad and Sam ducked his head against the blizzard with the rest of them.

First period was religious studies. The class was known among the students as a "doss" and Sam had no problem excusing himself at the start of the lesson as planned. "Sir, Mr Lonigan, sir? Might I run back to the house, sir? I've left my homework diary."

"Go on, then. Be quick about it," the teacher replied, without looking up.

Sam was out of the room in a shot, before anyone could object or say anything which might delay him. He threaded through the lines filing into classrooms and skipped down the gritted steps. This was the nerviest part of the journey, for he was effectively standing out from the crowd, but if anyone stopped him now he was prepared to lie and say he was being sent again for photo-copies. But nobody saw him. Nobody stopped him. And as soon as he was inside the Main Building he knew he was in with a chance of success – but he also knew he had to be quick; time was short.

Straining his ears for squeaking floorboards or squealing hinges, Sam took off his own jumper to reveal the one he'd stolen from matron's storeroom which belonged to Eddie Burroughs. Balling his own and leaving it hidden on the top of the glass cases outside the staffroom, Sam wandered down to the closed door of The Eleusinian Room and pressed his ear to the oak door.

Yes!

There were noises inside. That meant the cleaner was in there and, Sam hoped, it also meant he was about to come out just as he had done the day before.

Sam busied himself again in front of the boards. He nodded at the drama teacher, Mrs Donelley, who seemed to burst through the back door in her hurry to get into the staffroom. Although she'd only spied him momentarily through her red-framed crazy glasses, Sam knew she'd start asking questions if she saw him again when she came out, so he hid around the corner by the open fire and prayed she'd go straight back out the way she'd come.

She did.

As the staffroom door swung closed Sam heard a raspy, phlegmy cough from the same corridor and slid around the polished corner to call out, "Just a minute, please, sir!"

The cleaner, unshaven and grumpy-looking, kicked his dirty mop bucket out of The Eleusinian Room. "Whaddya want?"

Sam arrived, puffing. "Sorry, sir. It's just that Mrs Bainbridge said one of the girls has been sick on the carpet outside Mrs

Water's office, sir. It's the Governor's meeting today and Mrs Waters asked if you could go up there now and do whatever you could. She said it's a bit of an emergency, sir."

The cleaner was obviously torn between being offended at having to actually do something and being flattered that the Headmistress had asked for him. He forced a tired-sounding sigh from his dry lips and took out his key chain. "No rest for the wicked, I see."

"Ah, could I just nip in there?" Sam tried, pointing at the crack in the door behind the man's back. "I left my tie in there yesterday, sir. During The Magistrate's meeting. I've been sent to get it."

The cleaner's eyes, as Sam knew they would, flickered down to the badge sewn into the jumper he was wearing. "Quick as you can, then."

"Thing is –" Sam shrugged – "I'm not a hundred per cent sure where I left it." Sam pulled an apologetic face. "I might be a couple of minutes."

"Well, make sure you close the bleeding door over when you leave," the cleaner growled, already moving off. "I'll lock it proper when I come back." He shook his head as he walked away. "Knew it was going to be one of those days today."

Sam let the door of The Eleusinian Room close behind himself and felt for a light. Something flickered high up in the ceiling and the room lit up. The parquet floor was gleaming with mop whorls and smelled intoxicatingly clean.

Sam walked across to the nearest wall and pulled back the thin, linen curtain which hung from ceiling to floor. This revealed a series of plaques and a quantity of stacked books, mostly old ledgers, whose leather spines poked out towards him. Each was embossed with a date. 1878, 1879, 1880…

In the middle of the same wall, so high up that Sam had to take a squelching step backwards on the parquet to see it, there was an inlaid altar with a large book set on a golden stand.

That has to be a reproduction of The Book, Sam thought.

On either side of the golden stand, just as Eddie Burroughs had described it during their walk, there were two small, dusty blue bottles. *The ashes of the other two books the old lady wanted to sell!* Above these was the school shield and higher yet, folded against the wall, the Union Jack and the school flag.

Sam turned to the remainder of the room. There was a raised stage, a lectern and some stacked chairs but his eyes were drawn to the library which spiralled up into the ceiling above his head. The lowest shelves, packed with books, hung just out of reach and wound upwards over three floors to a small dome where lime-green light streamed in through a circle of stained-glass windows.

Sam walked across the slightly giving floor until he stood right underneath a steel walkway which he could touch if he jumped and stretched his arm. He could see the shelves and books twirling upwards and knew he had to somehow get up into the cage-like structure and have a look at what there was.

The stage was empty but for a chair and some cables but Sam noticed there was a grate near the other wall which he knew would contain either a storage space or pipes. Kneeling on the floor, peering down through the brass holes, he made out the glinting outline of some sort of music instrument and, tugging the grate up, quickly saw what he was looking for: the long, hook-ended rod he needed to pull down the bottom set of stairs which would give him access to the secret Magistrate-controlled library.

Sam had to climb into the hole under the grate to get the rod. There was an odd smell in the air, of burning or charring, and when he climbed back out into the room he found his shoes and fingertips were sooty. He set to work on hooking down the staircase unaware that he had just been inside the school's book-burning pit. This was where, during meetings of the High Magistrate, banned books were deposited and destroyed.

The staircase swung down as he pulled it with the rod and Sam quickly clanged up the rungs to the first floor. The tightly packed books on the shelves were modern here and there were even catalogues listing books available in electronic formats. Sam looked up – there were two more floors – before glancing back to the main door.

How long do I have?

He ran up a narrow, twirling set of steel steps to the next floor and began again quickly scanning the shelves. There seemed to be no rhyme or reason to the order of the books stored here and Sam thought, *I'll start at the top, with the old ones, and work my way down.* So he went up again, puffing as he turned and twisted on the steel rungs until he finally came out on a small platform where the stained glass windows surrounded him and cast his skin green. Crouching, he could see the glow of the snow without, and some cars, but the old glass was too thick and the windows too dirty to see more.

Keep your mind on the books.

The tomes whose spines he ran his fingers along now were ancient: battered red and bruised brown. There were rolled maps and yellowing scrolls laid on top of the volumes themselves and in some places the books seemed to have been shovelled into the shelves two and three deep. Sam didn't know where to start. He read the titles with mounting anxiety, not sure what he was looking for, when his eyes were drawn to a familiar name. *Leana: The Lost Princess*, the spine read. "Leana?"

Sam pulled out the thin but stocky volume. The sheets were thick, crisp, pungent and yellow.

O' hurry hard, O' hurry see
She fades as fast as night
To where o' where the dreamer's dream
To where the sleepers sigh.

Sam closed the book.

Is this about my Leana? No, of course not. Why would it be?

He thought about tucking the book inside his jumper but decided it would be too risky.

I need to come back here. With more time.

He looked down and knew he had to go. Perhaps he would try to be elected into The Magistrate, like Eddie. Then perhaps he could come in here whenever he wanted? And wasn't there an activity, Rectification or Rehabilitation or something like that, where you actually came and took care of the books? He'd heard something about it.

Sam couldn't get the Leana poems back into their space and bent to see why. A folded paper had fallen across the space the volume had occupied. Sam plucked it out and the other book slid straight in. Despite the screaming in his head telling him to escape while the coast was clear, Sam couldn't resist unfolding the paper.

It was a hand-drawn map.

It was difficult to see what it was showing at first but Sam picked out a cross with SC inked beside it which he took to be St Catherine's Church. From the cross there was a dotted line which read 'route'. This snaked its way across the paper to an 'x' and beside the 'x' were shapes indicating, Sam thought, a plan of a room. Almost immediately it became obvious to him that he was looking at was a plan of Mrs Water's office. The windows were marked, as were the fireplace, the door and the secretary's office. The only other mark on the map was a small diagram of a book and a scrawl: *Sybil's Tome.*

Folding the paper and threading it in beside the Leana book, Sam thought, *This is the route of a tunnel or a path which goes from the church to the school – to Water's office. The tunnel joins the chimney somewhere under the school. That must be the way in.* His eyes stared down at the grate on the floor of The Eleusinian Room. *The book Mr Chipping told us about must be up there. Sybil's book. The School Book! In Water's office!*

With a jarring squeal the main wooden door of The Eleusinian

Room creaked open. Sam ducked and saw the cleaner's bald head through the steel bars. He was with someone Sam couldn't see. There were two pairs of footsteps.

The had cleaner run into the centre of the room and now, spying Sam on the highest landing, he pointed up and screamed, "There he is! I've got him! He's still here! He's up there, caught like a rat! I see him!"

21

Extract from Leana: The Lost Princess

Between the worlds of peace and war
Love and hate
A queen to be
Huddles, waits
The church doors close
The heath in rain
A baby lain
Wrapped in Hope
and Fate

Destined for worlds of war and peace
Love and hate
A witch's gift
Time's portal wide
The future waits
The past behind
A prince is born
A curse waylaid
Good and Evil
Thrice betrayed

Above and beyond war and peace
Sublimity
And life's a dream
A princess cries a salty stream
Innocence wrapped in meaning
Finders keepers
Love and belief
The moon's baleful eye

The princess dreams
The past alive
A king's last cry
The basic law
Which underlies
Power, Magic, Destiny
Truth and Lies
Right Mind
Right Mind
Right Action sends
A sign.

The princess made of stars and dust
Rises like her mother sun
Drinks the water which took her blood
And sings a song that lover's love.

22

Knowledge Is Power

Sam was walking into Mrs Water's office again, the same fire roaring in the grate, watching Mrs Waters standing up and smiling and nodding at him just like the last time. Behind her the curtains were drawn: purple velvet, roof to floor, strangling all the light to death. Did she know he knew who she was?

"Well, well, Mr Lawrence. What are we going to do with you?"

Sam felt light-headed. He wasn't sure what had happened. The clock on the wall showed it was late afternoon. "Did I faint?"

"Yes. But you have been revived. You were in The Eleusinian Room." Mrs Waters unscrewed a fat fountain pen and beginning to fill in the blanks on the form she had in front of her. Sam couldn't help noticing the graphic in the bottom right corner of the page. A full moon.

Of course. This is the day. Today is the full moon. The last blink of Selene's eye. Today, when I fall asleep, I shall see Leana again. All this will be resolved.

"Are you not even going to try and explain yourself?" Waters asked, disgusted.

"I can't remember anything, miss," Sam began. "Maybe the cleaner? Perhaps I tripped over his bucket? Or maybe the fumes of that stuff he uses overwhelmed me and I fainted? I really couldn't say."

"Fumes? Overwhelmed?" Mrs Waters shook her head and tutted. "Mr Lawrence, perhaps I should tell you that how you came to be in The Eleusinian Room is the least of your problems. No, no. Theft! Yes, the theft of a jersey belonging to an invested Quaestor, is the truly shocking part of all this. That and subterfuge! The use of this stolen property to facilitate your entrance into a..."

And on it went.

Sam bowed his head, pretending to be sorry for all he had done but in reality looking down at the reflection in his watch face to scan the mantelpiece and the room behind him. He moved his wrist to take in the back wall.

"Which is why we've informed, at great difficulty with no little reluctance, your father about all of this and why, first thing tomorrow, you shall be picked up by your uncle and taken away from the school."

"What?"

Mrs Water's unscrewed her fountain pen and began writing. "As you know, I had an agreement with both you and your guardian regarding your comportment here at the school. Despite my efforts, this worrying behaviour of yours has recurred and this recurrence has provoked the course of action I'm now sadly forced to follow. Your father and your uncle are both in agreement that St Francis's is not the best environment for you at this present moment as we're all of the opinion that –" she glanced up, batting her dark eye-lashes – "you're not a very well little boy."

"And you're Hecate, the Queen of the witches," Sam almost replied. But he didn't. He didn't because some speedy mental gymnastics reminded him that he still had a night left. Uncle Quentin was coming tomorrow; *tomorrow first thing*, Waters had just said. In one night he could sort this thing out. He would go to wherever Leana was, or Leana would come here, they would resolve the issue and that would be that.

"Do you mind if I go now, miss? I'd like a drink of water and a lie down."

"Very well. I've informed Mr Dahl of what we've decided. You're excused Prep. Spend the time you have left tonight packing, please."

"Yes, miss. Thank you, miss."

"Can I trust you to make it back to the House alone without any further mishaps?"

"Yes, miss."

"Very well, then. Off you go."

Sam walked out to find Katy and her friend waiting on the landing. "Did you get expelled?" tall Katy asked. Sam nodded and heard them both run into the girl's common room and announce, "Lawrence got kicked out!"

In the time it took him to walk out of the back door of the Main Building and wander around to St Nick's, Katy had opened a window and shouted the news across the driveway to some boys sitting on a bench outside the house. When Sam walked in through the locker room door, everyone knew.

He spent the two hours of Prep packing his things, the only awkward moment coming when Eddie Burroughs came in just before the bell and asked him why he'd stolen his jumper. "And why did you have to drag me into all this?" Burroughs asked, hurt.

"Sorry, man. I needed the badge."

"I thought it was all secret, what we said?"

"It was. I didn't tell them anything about you."

"You didn't have to." As he was leaving Burroughs stopped at the door and said, "You need to get your head sorted, man. Seriously."

Sam stayed on his own until lights out. He lay facing the wall, already in bed, as the others came in. There was little conversation but when the lights went off Walt's voice struck up. "Well, it was nice knowing you, Sammo, mate. Be careful out there."

"Take care, Sammo," came another voice.

"Be good."

"Lucky sod."

"Selfish idiot."

When the voices stopped and the owl's hoots began, Sam lay waiting to sleep. But Orhan had a cough. And Simon Stainrod in

Dorm Five was snivelling so loud it was like he was standing next to Sam and shouting down his ear. The Hindi sleep-talker chose that night, at about two, to begin reciting verses of the Bhagavad Gita in his dreams – "*I am death! The creator of worlds!*" – and Little Billy Astbury in Dorm One had a four o'clock nightmare and screamed the house down, wailing about wolves and motorbikes.

But just before dawn, when he wasn't expecting it, as usual, Sam dropped off.

23

Believe That Life Is Worth Living And Your Belief Will Help Create The Fact

Leana was chained to something that felt like snakeskin.

The noise around her was pitiful and terrifying: screams of pain and cries for mercy. Shadows hung on either side, limbs shaking their chains while grime covered the floor like a brown sea. But she was alive! Why had the giant chained her to this slimy wall instead of killing her? Something had made him panic.

There was one window in the dungeon, high up. It generated a beam of divine light which cut across the smudged, bleak interior space as though solid. Sometimes a prisoner might pop up in the silver line, eyes bulging, teeth missing, and try to eat or drink it. Whips cracked and doors squealed. A woman was laughing manically.

A hole in the wall opposite Leana burst open with blinding light. Leana felt and then saw a great blade poised above her head and screamed with the little energy she had left. But there was no pain and no blow. Instead she felt a series of hot sparks burn the soft skin on the insides of her wrists and a moment later she fell to the filthy floor.

On hands and knees, she heard someone bellow, "Every man, woman and child in this wretched, ungodly hive of sin is hereby freed and ordered to fight for and defend the rightful King, their liberator, for the love of God and country!"

Someone grabbed Leana's shoulders and hoisted her to her feet. "Stand up and fight, girl! You are liberated!"

"Traitor!" came a voice from behind, in the light, and a fight broke out.

Leana joined the reeking, heaving mass surging to escape.

They passed through the doorway in the wall and came out into a cold gale blowing over the balustrades. They were on a long passageway open to the elements and Leana joined the others in taking in the countryside as though it was their first ever view of the earth.

"Hark!" a scared voice cried. "The wood's moving!"

"'Tis Malcolm!"

Leana watched as Birnam Wood in the distance did indeed seem to move forwards, the great green mushrooms of the tree canopies bobbing in step to the soldiers supporting them. Her heart fluttered like the standards she spotted between the boughs. Down below Macbeth's troops were hurriedly digging earth works and forming defensive lines of archers.

"My daughter! My daughter!"

"Make way for the Queen! Make way for the Queen!"

Leana stood on tiptoes and, looking down upon the walkway below, caught the eye of a pale, worried looking Lady Macbeth staring upwards. Her skin was an unhealthy grey. Behind her, his expensive French cloak flapping in the wind, stood the doctor. Leana ducked back onto her own balustrade and began pushing through the prisoners. She heard a cry from below. "My daughter! I saw her! Up there! Catch her!"

Leana ran back to the open dungeon. It was empty of bodies but skittering with rats. She needed a place to hide. Was there another way out?

Standing in the centre of the chamber she noticed darker than normal shadows near the bottom of the walls and skidded across to investigate. She almost cried out with joy when she found holes and small indents which must have been dug and scraped out by prisoner's fingernails.

"My child!" Lady Macbeth's voice echoed through the dungeon and scared a small colony of bats somewhere in the high roof. They swooped, squealed and flapped out above and around the Queen's head. "Where are you?"

Leana crushed herself into the largest of the cavities and immediately felt something warm, furry and alive inside with her. The living thing growled. Not loudly, but softly, as a warning. "Please allow me to share this space with you," Leana whispered. "I promise I will look after you or do whatever you want when I get out of here, even though I know you can't understand a word I'm saying."

"My darling! Come back to me! Come to me!"

The bundle of fur pressing against her was a dog. Leana knew it by the way it licked her nose. The smell of it. She opened her eyes and pushed herself further into the sunken hole the dog allowed her to enter and together they crouched in the dank pit.

"If she's in here, find her!" the Queen demanded of her closest guard. The sweet, slightly mad, cooing voice she'd been using changed. "Find the wretch and drag her out to me!" Her voice was horrible now, as though she were gargling bile. "How dare she play games with me!"

Leana, buried with Camilo the dog, her back to the dungeon, closed her eyes against the spiky fur and listened to the sploshing and squelching and lunging and huffing of the brutes sent in to find her. Some noises sounded too close for comfort but Leana was soothed by the calmness of her canine companion. The dog hardly moved. She could hear its steadily beating heart beside her ear and loved it.

"They've breached the moat, ma'am!" a worried, echoing voice cried out.

"She's not here, ma'am!" another voice shouted, closer.

The Queen's banshee shriek made Leana's teeth hurt and the dog shake.

When she could sense it was safe to do so, Leana eased her way out and beckoned for the dog to come with her. "Come on, boy. I'll give you whatever you want." But Camilo was adamant he didn't want to move. He remained at the mouth of the small cave, tongue lolled out, dropping his head whenever she caught his eye. Leana kissed his wet button nose and left.

She stayed close to the wall as she edged towards the doorway, ready to hide at any time. Occasional arrows came skittering down the dungeon steps and stuck in the mud while great battering noises shook dust from the ceiling. The omnipresent crackle of flames grew as Leana emerged onto the battlements again, now shrouded in thick, acrid smoke. When it cleared she caught a glimpse of the full moon hanging low over the stubs of Birnam, watching the chaos like a baleful, monophthalmic god.

Leana became aware of a body tumbling through the air from the battlements above her – a woman's body – and in the brief second it took to pass she recognised the Queen's clothing. Looking down over the edge of the grey stone she saw long ladders being slapped into place against the walls. Between them there was a huddle on the ground around a lady staring up to the sky with dead eyes. An odd white imitation of the queen floated out of the body and vanished upwards into the smoke above the mourners and Leana was overcome by a premonition that finally – as it just had done for the Queen – everything was about to end.

"Die, traitor!" A man in armour was charging towards her with a lance. "Prepare to meet your master!"

Although people were being speared and thrown from the walls on either side of her like rubbish, and although there were fireballs rising in plumes to her left and tar being emptied down upon whoever was climbing up the ladders, Leana found herself very calm and composed of mind. In fact, she thought of the dog. That poor dog. Up to its neck in dirt and filth. But swimming in it. Not drowning. *Who will take care of that lovely dog? And why does he not want to escape?*

"Leana!"

A familiar voice. "Sam?"

In his eyes – for it was Sam, as Robbie, running towards her in the opposite direction as the man with the lance, with the sky at his back and blood splashed across his face – Leana saw love. He had come back to save her. He had reunited with the Thane's army. He had marched on the castle. Macbeth would be defeated. Scotland would once again be at peace! But in the same moment Leana froze with horror as she realised that Sam was going to die.

Sam grabbed Leana by the shoulders and turned her out of the path of the onrushing soldier. Their eyes met in a wordless, deep connection which seemed to freeze time. But then the lance meant for Leana pierced Sam's chest, killing him instantly and, after staggering a moment, he dropped to the stone in a crumpled, bloody heap.

Leana fell sideways into the arms of the Queen's chambermaid who rushed them both away through the thickest part of the smoke to the stairwell. There were arrows poking out of door but it opened at a stiff kick from the chambermaid's clog. She dragged Leana inside through the sticky, drying tar that was steaming off the steps.

"Is it over?" asked Leana as they came out into the courtyard. Malcolm's soldiers were swarming the castle now and hoisting their flag from the tower.

"The King is dead!" a figure yelled from the roof of the keep.

"Long live the King!" came the shouted reply from the castle gate, where Malcolm came striding in with his elite troops.

"Yes, my dear," the chambermaid said. "It's all over."

24

Dreams Are True While They Last and Do We Not Live In Dreams?

"The uncle swore he'd be here by ten."

"I can't wait anymore."

"I can. Don't worry, I'll stay, you go."

"Keep this door securely locked."

"Oh, don't you worry about that."

"Ah, one thing before I go. Do we know anything about the father?"

"Flying back from the desert this afternoon. The uncle said he'll have the boy until then. The father knows someone, apparently. A decent doctor."

"Same one who's treating the mother?"

"Perhaps they'll get a family deal?"

Sam opened one eye. He tried to move but was immobile. Had he broken every bone in his body? No. He was restrained. Lying face up.

"I'm surprised the boy lasted being out all night in this weather."

"But that's the thing, you see. If he wasn't aware of it, there's a good chance that he hardly noticed. He could have thought he was anywhere."

"But the cold's the cold, Malcolm."

"He's just lucky he decided to bed down in the church. He could have really gone walkabout – been hit by a car, or anything. Sleepwalkers are a liability to themselves."

Sam wriggled the restraints off his feet and this gave him purchase to slide out from under the straps which wrapped him to the bed. Now he could see where he was: Sick Bay again. *This place is like my second home.*

Obviously the teachers in the corridor were talking about him but Sam didn't care. He lifted his pyjama top and stared down at his chest. No hole. No wound. But he remembered everything from Scotland. *That* part he remembered. But sleeping outside? In the church? The last thing he could remember here, at the school, was the coughing, snivelling and talking last night. The endless noise. But he'd slept, hadn't he?

There was nothing there, when he thought back. A void.

But in Scotland he'd seen Leana and she had been alive.

I must keep going. I must get out of here. He thought of the map he'd seen in The Eleusinian Room and decided, *I will get into Water's office. If The Book is anywhere, it's there.*

As quietly as he could, Sam slipped off the bed. The springs creaked but the voices outside continued conversing: now they were talking about Sam's mother, the writer, and her mysterious disappearance. It was Mr Dahl and, Sam thought, Mr Seneca, the senior boy's housemaster.

Sam stuffed the bed as best he could to make it look as though he was still lying beneath the sheets before going over to the pile of damp clothes on the chair by the door. He needed his shoes and jacket: everything else could wait.

Creeping over to the window, Sam examined the panes. There was one large window which had been secured with a combination padlock. It wouldn't budge. The small, narrow top-window was ajar, just as it had been when he'd first come here with Pram.

He heard the Indonesian's voice in his mind. What had he said? *Close the window if you want to get out of here.*

Close it? Feeling slightly mad, Sam pulled the small window closed and stepped back. He half expected some kind of magic to happen but nothing occurred. The room became very warm very quickly: the clinking radiators under the windows were working at full power.

Sam considered trying to break the glass, to throw something through it, but a moment later he began to laugh. As the windows had steamed up the panes revealed a three-digit number.

Close window if you want to get out, he heard Pram say again.

"Thanks, mate!"

Sam tried the three digits on the combination lock. They worked. He was out.

Sam was an animal, crouched, hustling; a Yeti; a ghost.

He moved from car to car along the school drive, crouching in the bracken and behind the drifts as vehicles bringing in the day bugs slid past through the slush.

The bell rang for Assembly and it sounded faraway and strange. He waited three minutes, counting out the seconds, and then began moving up towards the school buildings via the narrow pathway between the tennis courts and the sixth form block. He peeped up into the first window he passed and was happy to see the study cubicle was unoccupied. The tennis courts were empty too, streaked with icy puddles, the nets sagging, torn and sad.

At the edge of the sixth form block Sam saw the fire escape door of the Assembly Hall and watched green-jumpered students filing by inside. A Praetor was standing with his back to the window, arms linked behind his back and Sam hated him. If he ever had any power over this school that would be another thing he'd change: no more Magistrate! What where the Quaestors, Praetors and Consuls, anyway, but Hecate's guards? They unwittingly and willingly maintained all that was wrong with the school while thinking they were doing right, the dumb, deluded, power-hungry fools!

The snow had begun to fall again, heavy and thick. It would settle.

Sam darted from his hiding place and ran across to where four paths intersected. He stuck close to the peeling yellow fence outside the kitchens and ran bent over. A kitchen porter was pushing a bin out of the back door and a radio was playing pop music inside. Sam moved on, out towards the front lawn and along the façade of the Main Building. He kept his back close to the ivory-strewn wall, ready to bolt or hide at any moment.

He glanced across at St Nick's and wondered if his escape had been noticed. The dark windows stared back at him. The great oak tree reached up into the dark, marble sky. All was quiet.

Now he was in the main door and running past the fire in the front hall, sprinting up the stairs alongside panels filled with golden lettering. The stairs creaked but he raced on, reaching the green carpet, in sight of his target. A moment later, in front of a sign which read "MRS WATERS: HEADMISTRESS" he stopped for breath.

Now what?

As he leaned back against the door, sweating, realising he needed to find a spare key – perhaps it would be in the secretary's office? – the door clicked open behind him and he had to spin quickly to catch it and stop it banging off the inside wall.

Sam ducked inside, closing the door, and walked past the fire to Water's desk and looked out through the bay windows. He could see the back lawns, the playing fields and, through the snow, sometimes, the hills. Closer, down below, he saw the Assembly Hall, packed but silent.

I'm here. I'm in here. Search!

Sam started with the desk. Two of the drawers were locked but the longest, which ran the entire length of the writing surface, slid open to reveal a mobile phone, some keys, a black purse and a pair of scissors. Sam slammed it shut and looked up. There were some books on a shelf behind the sofa at the furthest end of the room, near the door, and some objects dotted about on the mantelpiece above the fire. He decided to try the mantelpiece first.

Sam didn't know what to make of the objects he saw. There was a two-headed foetus, an animal of some kind, floating in aspic or liquid. The eyes stared out at Sam and gave him the creeps. Next were a collection of small off-white objects arranged on a brass plate: again Sam got a shiver when he realised he was looking at teeth. The teeth of *what*, exactly, he wasn't sure.

Check the bookcase. Stay awake. Stay alert.

To read the titles on the spines of the books Sam had to put one hand on the corner of the frame but all the titles began to swim before his eyes and he suddenly heard the books talking to him: the words of each book were being spoken in his own voice – but the timbre and tone of each of his voices was different.

He could make out his normal voice, the voice he heard inside his own head, the same voice he'd always heard inside his own head, but he could also hear other tones and accents. He heard himself talking as a baby. Heard his voice as he read in class – that horrible self-conscious monotone. He heard his recorded voice. His happy voice. Acting the fool. Taking the mickey. Somewhere else he was crying, upset.

Sam fell to the floor and held his ears.

Give up Sam! he heard.

Don't give up, Sam!

He made himself stand up and ran to the window, wanting air, but his eyes immediately focussed on Mrs Waters who was walking across the snow in the centre of the back lawn. Her fresh footsteps, strangely sooty, trailed back to the Assembly Hall. Behind her the students were oozing out of the Hall exits like green blood. Water's eyes were glowing red and her face, which Sam knew only he could see, had taken on a terrible aspect, as though she were hundreds of years old. *Finally she reveals herself!*

Turning back to the room Sam saw the walls were bare, very white and that he was standing on brown, unpolished floor-boards. The hearth was black and empty and there was a man walking towards Sam with a book in his hand and a dog by his side. The man smiled and Sam recognised him as Mr Chipping.

Sam took the book as it was offered but as he touched it everything vanished. There was a crash of thunder and he was back in the stuffy room, back with the fire and curtains and dizziness and a ceiling alive with flapping bats wings.

Sam was knocked down and a terrible, powerful force began to drag him by the feet towards the fireplace, towards the flames in the grate which had taken on the appearance of a fiery-orange, gaping jaw.

So this is how it ends.

The grip on his shoes was so fierce that Sam lay back on the carpet and put his hands behind his head and surrendered. He knew he couldn't die again – he had done that once, to save Leana – but now he must find out why he was here and why he had been pitted against Hecate. He must find out how this ended.

Sam was calm. He wanted the magic over. He wanted to know reality.

As the leather on his toecaps hissed, popped and melted in the jaws of the fire, Sam looked up, half-hoping to see angels or perhaps some kindly old relative telling him everything was going to be all right, but instead noticed the portrait of the Mr Chipping and his dog hanging over the fire. The painting was wavy, affected by the heat from the flames below and he thought at that moment he could hear the old master's voice saying, *You have the power, Sam. Use The Book. End Hecate's reign. She has been waiting for one who has the power. Use what is within you before she uses you. Use the power within.*

"Within. Within."

In a moment Sam had kicked off his shoes, jumped up and punched through the canvas. His arm came back with a wide old book clenched inside his bleeding knuckles and Sam knew it was the prize: so that was where the book had been kept!

And as the bats came down and the fire leapt from the grate, the Queen of Witches appeared transfigured by brilliant light in the doorway. Sam flipped open the great book on the desk and the teeth chattered on their bronze trays, the jewels which made up the sand in the windows melted, the hairs and nails in the dirt of the carpet twitched and chattered and the insects in the sofa coughed blood.

Ignoring the inferno all around him, Sam began to write.

25

The Beginning And The End Of A Circle Are One

Dear Saraswati,

Thank you so much for your letter! Of course I'd be happy to be your pen-pal and write to you from time to time. I love knowing about other cultures and would like to know all about your country and where you live.

At the moment I go to a school in the middle of the countryside here in England. It's called St Francis's and it is a boarding school for girls and boys. I miss my parents a lot but luckily I have my sister, Gemma, here. Maybe I'll tell you about her in another letter.

I have many friends even though I've only been here a month or so. My best friends are Gillian, Kizzie and Charlotte. Our housemistress is a nice lady called Mrs Bainbridge who tells us incredible stories at night. We live in the Main Building, which is very old and full of secret passages and legends. Maybe in the next letter I'll tell you one of them?

The headmaster here is a nice man called Mr Firmin. He likes sailing a lot and is trying to change the tennis courts into a big boating lake but nobody else seems too keen. The Head Boy and Head Girl this year are Sam and Leana They are really nice and both of them take good care of all the new pupils to make sure they settle in. We see them a lot because Sam's mother is a famous writer and she is a friend of Miss Bainbridge.

In school I take all the usual subjects. In biology we are studying plants and cells, in English *Romeo and Juliet* and in geography, coastal erosion. I like all the subjects but my favourite activity is drama. This year, for the first time, I've got a part in the end of year play. More details to follow!

I wish I could write more but I have to go to bed now. Please write and tell me how you are. Tell me about your family and your school and what you do. Do you have any good legends in your town? Any mysteries? I like mysteries. Tell me about the weather there and what you eat. I would love to know everything.

I hope you like writing. I do!

Speak soon. Lots of love,
Athena.

About the Author

James was born on a rainy Thursday in the north of England in May, 1973. Six years later he moved with his family to the heat and humidity of Singapore before experiencing a wet couple of years on the rugged east coast of Scotland, near Aberdeen. He went to a boarding school not dissimilar to St Francis de Sales before going on to university in London.

For most of his twenties James wandered about Ireland, France, Germany and Thailand, washing dishes, making sandwiches, watching various world cups and teaching English.

He now lives in Madrid, Spain, with his wife and two children.

James would like to thank Han, Matso, Seets, Ben, Paul, Dan, Kim, Car, Pepe, Jon, Luce and Max for their help, hospitality and advice in writing this book. Thanks also to everyone at Lodestone and JHP. Thank you, too, for reading it.

About Shakespeare's Moon

The Invisible Hand is the first in the *Shakespeare's Moon* series of books about St Francis de Sales school and the adventures of the people who go there.

If you would like to find out more about the other books in the series, have a chance of appearing in the next book as a character or take part in other exciting competitions, go to jameshartleybooks.com for more information, or follow us on Facebook or Twitter.

LODESTONE BOOKS

Lodestone Books

YOUNG ADULT FICTION

Lodestone Books is a new imprint, which offers a broad spectrum of subjects in YA/NA literature. Compelling reading, the Teen/Young/New Adult reader is sure to find something edgy, enticing and innovative. From dystopian societies, through a whole range of fantasy, horror, science fiction and paranormal fiction, all the way to the other end of the sphere, historical drama, steam-punk adventure, and everything in between (including crime, coming of age and contemporary romance). Whatever your preference you will discover it here. If you have enjoyed this book, why not tell other readers by posting a review on your preferred book site. Recent bestsellers from Lodestone Books are:

AlphaNumeric

Nicolas Forzy
When dyslexic teenager Stu accidentally transports himself into a world populated by living numbers and letters, his arrival triggers a prophecy that pulls two rival communities into war.
Paperback: 978-1-78279-506-3 ebook: 978-1-78279-505-6

Shanti and the Magic Mandala

F.T. Camargo

In this award-winning YA novel, six teenagers from around the
world gather for a frantic chase across Peru, in search of a
sacred object that can stop The Black Magicians' final plan.
Paperback: 978-1-78279-500-1 ebook: 978-1-78279-499-8

Time Sphere

A timepathway book
M.C. Morison

When a teenage priestess in Ancient Egypt connects with a
schoolboy on a visit to the British Museum, they each come
under threat as they search for Time's Key.
Paperback: 978-1-78279-330-4 ebook: 978-1-78279-329-8

Bird Without Wings FAEBLES

Cally Pepper

Sixteen-year-old Scarlett has had more than her fair share of
problems, but nothing prepares her for the day she discovers
she's growing wings...
Paperback: 978-1-78099-902-9 ebook: 978-1-78099-901-2

Briar Blackwood's Grimmest of Fairytales

Timothy Roderick

After discovering she is the fabled Sleeping Beauty, a brooding
goth-girl races against time to undo her deadly fate.
Paperback: 978-1-78279-922-1 ebook: 978-1-78279-923-8

Escape from the Past
The Duke's Wrath

Annette Oppenlander
Trying out an experimental computer game, a fifteen-year-old
boy unwittingly time-travels to medieval Germany where he
must not only survive but figure out a way home.
Paperback: 978-1-84694-973-9 ebook: 978-1-78535-002-3

Holding On and Letting Go

K.A. Coleman
When her little brother died, Emerson's life came crashing down
around her. Now she's back home and her friends want to help,
but can Emerson fight to re-enter the world she abandoned?
Paperback: 978-1-78279-577-3 ebook: 978-1-78279-576-6

Midnight Meanders

Annika Jensen
As William journeys through his own mind, revelations are
made, relationships are broken and restored, and a faith that
once seemed extinct is renewed.
Paperback: 978-1-78279-412-7 ebook: 978-1-78279-411-0

Reggie & Me

The First Book in the Dani Moore Trilogy
Marie Yates
The first book in the Dani Moore Trilogy, Reggie & Me explores
a teenager's search for normalcy in the aftermath of rape.
Paperback: 978-1-78279-723-4 ebook: 978-1-78279-722-7

Unconditional

Kelly Lawrence
She's in love with a boy from the wrong side of town...
Paperback: 978-1-78279-394-6 ebook: 978-1-78279-393-9

Readers of ebooks can buy or view any of these bestsellers
by clicking on the live link in the title. Most titles are published
in paperback and as an ebook. Paperbacks are available in
traditional bookshops. Both print and ebook formats are
available online.

Find more titles and sign up to our readers' newsletter at
http://www.johnhuntpublishing.com/children-and-young-adult.
Follow us on Facebook at
https://www.facebook.com/JHPChildren
and Twitter at https://twitter.com/JHPChildren.